A Life Interrupted

By: A.K. Roberts

A Life Interrupted – the Prequel

Text copyright © 2016 by A.K. Roberts

For information visit:
A.K.Roberts.com

ISBN 978-0-9978047-0-6 (pbk)

First Edition: July 2016

10 9 8 7 6 5 4 3 2 1

A special thank you to my husband and children. My husband is the best man I know. He supports me, encourages me, keeps me grounded and makes all my dreams come true. My children are incredible and very supportive. Thank you for believing in me and being patient with me over the last two years.

CHAPTER ONE

Everything happens for a reason. No one could have predicted it, no one would have believed it or imagined it would involve so many people, but it's true and the ripple effects will be far-reaching, lives will be destroyed, and no one will see it coming or ever be the same.

A sociopath fears two things: losing control and being exposed.

July 4, 1955 was a day Maria Leonetti Donovan will never forget. Young and newly married, she was about to give birth to her first child at St. Matthew's Hospital, but there was one problem...her husband Patrick was not there yet.

Patrick Donovan got the call from Maria eighteen hours earlier, right before his last exam, and the moment it was over he ran out of class, jogged to his dorm, packed his bag, and ran for his car when his best friend Ben Beringer joined him.

"I'm coming with you!"

"No, man, I can't let you do that. You have exams."

Ben laughs and opens the door. "I think the birth of your first child is more important; besides you can't drive all that way by yourself. If I come with you, we can switch off and won't have to stop."

Patrick smiles. "Okay, let's go."

Driving through the night, only stopping when they had to, the friends drive from Annapolis, MD to Lake Forest, MO without incident.

Having known each other since their freshman year of high school at St. Louis College Prep in St. Louis, Ben and Patrick were like two peas in a pod. Both extremely intelligent, both patriotic, both extremely athletic they spent four years competing for the best grades, competing for the best sports stats and competing for the love of one girl, but Patrick won out in the end and Ben couldn't have been happier. Maria Leonetti was the sweetest, most beautiful girl they had ever known and it was obvious she was head over heels in love with Patrick from the moment she laid eyes upon him.

Cruising down the highway, meeting no interference, no traffic, Patrick thought for sure they were blessed. They were making great time and if it continued like this they would surely make it to Lake Forest in time, but there was something strange going on behind them, something both men noticed but never spoke about. There was a late model black sedan following them and had been since they left the Naval Academy at Annapolis.

Driving through the night, they ignored the black sedan, but at daybreak, Patrick couldn't take it anymore. He needed to talk to Maria, he needed to know how she was, how the baby was, so he decided to pull over and call the hospital. Pulling up to a gas station, he ran to the phone booth while Ben took care of pumping the gas and that's when he noticed the black sedan pull off the highway and follow them.

He should have said something, he should have talked to Ben about it, but the moment he heard Maria's voice nothing else mattered.

Panting hard, barely able to articulate a full sentence, Maria begged him to hurry.

"I am, sweetheart. I'm close," he replied. "I love you and I love that little baby, I'll be there and we will finally be a family. I'm not going back to school. I'm staying with you and our child."

The call ends and Maria reaches out to her grandmother, Francesca, clenches down on her hand and tries to breathe through the pain, but it's unbearable, it takes her breath away, and she isn't sure how much longer she can hold off from pushing.

Watching the clock, she counts the minutes between labor, tries to force her body to wait, but it's a losing battle. Frightened, scared, terrified, she cries out for Patrick, but he still hasn't arrived and for some reason she can't help but think something is wrong.

"Okay, Maria, push!" the doctor shouts.

"Patrick!" she screams.

At 4:10 AM tiny little Daniel Patrick Donovan takes his first breath at the same exact time his father, Patrick, takes his last.

"The car came out of nowhere, the driver never saw it coming, but this was no accident," bus driver Andy Bennett tells the Illinois Highway Trooper at 5AM the morning of July 4, 1955.

Patrick Donovan died at the scene. The driver, Ben Beringer, was in critical condition.

Weeks went by, it was touch and go, but Ben woke up from his coma on July 24, 1955 and his first question was "Where is Patrick?"

"He didn't make it," his mother reluctantly tells him.

"Oh god!"

Depressed and devastated, Ben blamed himself and when Maria finally came to see him he promised he would make things right, promised to take care of her and the baby and promised to do all of it in Patrick's name.

Four months later Maria agreed to marry Ben and even though the marriage was not rooted in love, Ben vowed to spend the rest of his life making good on his promises and devote his life to taking care of Maria and Patrick's son, Daniel.

Chapter Two

Daniel Patrick Beringer wanted for nothing, all the necessities and comforts of life were provided and always within reach. Safe and secure with two parents who loved him, Daniel knew he had a great life, everyone knew it, but looks can be deceiving.

There was something about his life that felt...wrong. Daniel didn't understand it and he would never talk to his mother about it, but he never felt close to his father, never felt the connection other boys felt. Ben was a good friend, but he never really felt like a father.

It wasn't until Daniel's junior year in high school when his English teacher assigned a research project that he would figure it out and when he did it would change his life forever.

Maria never told Daniel about Patrick Donovan, never even mentioned his name. Daniel never knew Ben Beringer wasn't his biological father, never questioned it, and as far as Maria was concerned that was exactly how she wanted it. Her life with Patrick died the day he died, she couldn't handle thinking about it and no matter how much time passed it was still too painful to talk about it, but secrets have a way of coming out when we least expect it and when they do they can change our lives forever.

"Mom, why do I have two birth certificates?" Daniel asks holding a piece of paper in both hands.

Maria's jaw drops. "How did you get those?"

"I was working on a research project for school, researching my family history, why do I have two birth certificates and who is Patrick Daniel Donovan?"

Stunned, speechless and emotional, Maria knew the time had finally come and after keeping this secret for seventeen years it was time to tell Daniel everything.

"Ben is not your biological father, Patrick Donovan was," Maria tearfully confesses to her son standing in front of her.

"What do you mean 'was'?"

"Patrick was killed in a car accident the day you were born."

4

Daniel's jaw drops. "So, Ben is not my father?"

She shakes her head. "No, Ben was Patrick's best friend, he was driving the car when a man driving a black sedan side-swiped them on the highway sent their car into a spin and Ben hit a concrete pier under a bridge. Patrick was ejected from the car, killed instantly; it was an accident."

For the first time in Daniel's life he is speechless.

"Ben was in a coma for weeks, when he finally regained consciousness he couldn't remember anything. It took him two months to recover enough to leave the hospital. He felt responsible and did everything in his power to try and make it right."

"How could he make it right?" Daniel asks, his voice rising.

"It wasn't his fault, Daniel. There were witnesses. Witnesses who saw the whole thing and testified. The police looked for the other driver, found the car abandoned alongside the highway in East St. Louis six hours after the accident, but the driver was gone. It is still an open investigation."

Hearing the news, everything in Daniel's life changed. He finally understood why he never felt close to Ben, he finally understood what was missing from his life and he wanted answers, so he set out to learn everything he could about Patrick Daniel Donovan, the accident which took Patrick's life and the driver who caused it.

Four years later, during his junior year in college, he finally solved the mystery, learned the whole truth, and armed with the knowledge that would finally bring his father's killer to justice he picked up the phone to call the Illinois State Trooper who had been helping him when he heard a knock at the door.

Opening the door, he was surprised to see his grandmother, Francesca standing there.

"Daniel, we need to talk," she said standing in front of him.

"Nonna, what are you doing here?"

"Sweetheart, I need you to stop this or at least hold off on doing anything until you hear me out. There are some things you need to know. Come on," she says and reaches for his arm. "Let's go for a walk."

Francesca Leonetti was beautiful, she had olive colored skin, dark brown hair, and dark brown eyes. She spoke with a slight Italian accent and she had a confidence he had never seen before. She was in charge, she knew it, and no one dared tell her otherwise.

"Your Mama has been through a lot, Daniel. She needs peace and so does your father, both your fathers," she says and looks at him. "Patrick was a great man, the best man I ever knew, and you remind me of him, you have the same personality," she says with a kind smile. "But Daniel, nothing is going to bring him back."

"I know."

"I know you've been investigating Patrick's death, I know you figured it out and I think you have an amazing future as an investigative journalist if that's the path you wish to be on, but I need you to keep this quiet."

"What?" Daniel asks sounding shocked. "But Nonna, I know who killed my father, I know who was driving that black sedan!"

Francesca turns to face her grandson. "I know you do. I know you figured out what happened. You're a natural investigator, you ask the right questions and you have a knack for putting all the pieces of a puzzle together, but I'm asking you to drop it, I'm asking you to keep it a secret...at least for now."

"Why?"

Francesca sighs. "Daniel, there will come a time when you will need this information, a time when you will need to have the upper hand and this information will give that to you."

He gives her a curious look. "But the man who killed Patrick is—

She holds up her hand and turns her head. "I know what you are going to say, I know who did it, but my loyalty lies with you...not him," she says and reaches for his hands. "Daniel, keep this quiet, hold on to it until you can use it. Believe me, there will come a time..."

"But—

"Trust me."

Daniel doesn't understand it, but something tells him to do what she says and he agrees to keep quiet.

A year later Daniel graduates Summa Cum Laude from the School of Journalism and advances to the Master's program where he is invited to partake in a high-profile internship at The Sun, a major publication in Washington D.C. where he lands the job of a lifetime.

Working for The Sun was always Daniel's dream. It was a nationally syndicated daily newspaper that had won more than a hundred Pulitzer Prizes and Daniel was determined to win the paper another.

Taking the pen name Daniel Donovan in honor of his biological father, it didn't take him long to make a name for himself. Daniel was a natural investigator, charming, and he had this knack for being in the right place at the right time. Bob, his editor, had never seen anything like it.

Life was good, Daniel was successful, but it wasn't enough. He was restless, restless for the story that would put his name on the lips of every person in the country, restless for the prize that eluded him, restless for the story that would break all stories.

Keeping an eye on the problems brewing in the Middle East, Daniel decided to call a meeting with Arthur Chadwick, the owner of The Sun, and discusses the possibility of becoming a foreign correspondent. Thinking the only way to get what he wanted was to follow this path, he convinced Chadwick to let him travel to Iran in the winter of 1988 to report on the growing problems between Iran and Iraq, but it didn't take long before those problems made international news and Daniel was right in the thick of it.

Stumbling upon an eyewitness account that Iraq was hiding weapons of mass destruction, Daniel set out to confirm his source and when he did he found himself thrust into the middle of the largest story of his life, but as the tensions between the two countries continued to mount and the threats from Hussein grew stronger the U.S. government decided it was too dangerous for him to stay and ordered him to leave.

"Daniel!" Bob, his editor, shouts. "I don't care if this is the biggest story on the planet! Saddam Hussein just sent a final warning to Iran. He is threatening to attack an Iranian city using weapons of mass destruction if they don't agree to his terms. You need to get out of there right now!"

Knowing Bob is right, knowing he is in the wrong place at the right time, Daniel flees the country, manages to get out just in time and as he boards a plane for Tel Aviv Hussein unleashes poison gas, kills 5,000 and leaves many more to die from their injuries.

Knowing how fortunate he was, Daniel calls his mother. He needs to hear her voice, he needs to reassure her he is okay and after he makes the call he boards a plane for D.C., meets a vivacious and very sexy blond flight attendant who will be taking care of all his needs on the way home, and leaves the chaos of the Middle East behind while he writes one of the greatest stories of his life.

Landing in D.C., Daniel has four things on his mind. One, to get the article he just wrote to his editor. Two, a nice juicy steak. Three, a long hot shower. Four, the vivacious blond for dessert.

Attractive and confident, Daniel commanded attention everywhere he went. Tall, with an athletic build, dark brown hair and navy blue eyes he looked like Cary Grant, but Daniel Beringer was more than a good-looking man. He was extremely intelligent and so charming he could swoon the Queen of England.

Daniel was every girl's dream.

Arriving in D.C. late in the evening he jumped into a cab with the blond, enjoyed the perfect steak, took a long, hot, sensual shower, and with the sultry sounds of Marvin Gaye in the background he was about to get what he wanted most when his phone rings for the third time since he got home.

Looking up for a moment, he considers answering it, but the blond has other plans and sliding her hands up his naked torso she gets his attention back.

Desire building, primal needs dominating his every thought, Daniel lowers himself back down, begins to trail kisses down her body to her belly and starts to move down between her legs when his phone rings again.

"What is going on?" he shouts and reaches over to grab the phone. "What?"

"Daniel, Bob!"

The blond flight attendant grabs the phone and ends the call, reaches up to grab Daniel and brings him back to where he was and as she arches her back, moans out loud and slides her fingers into his hair to clench tight the phone rings again, Daniel sits up, and diving for the phone he answers it for the last time.

"What?!" he shouts.

"Daniel, do not hang up on me again!"

"Bob?" he asks and sits up straighter. "Have you been calling me all night?"

"Yes! I need you to get back to the airport. There's been an incident and—

"Whoa, what?!" Daniel shouts and holds up his hands as if Bob can see him. "What incident? What are you talking about?"

Having been ignored long enough, the flight attendant sits up, grabs the cordless phone and tosses it on the floor. "Enough!" she shouts and grabs him to pull him back down. "I want you," she pants.

Forgetting about Bob for a moment, Daniel slowly lowers himself back down on top of her when he hears a faint mumble, sighs, and reaches for the phone. "Sorry, baby."

"DANIEL, WHAT THE HELL?!" Bob shouts.

Shocked, the blond flight attendant sits up. This has never happened to her before. "Can't this wait?" she asks sounding annoyed.

Bob hears her and exhales. "No, it can't wait—

Daniel laughs. "Fine, tell me what is going on."

"It's all over the news. There is a major story breaking down in the Caribbean."

"What? What story?"

"Daniel, I don't have time right now. I'll meet you at the airport in one hour," he says and ends the call.

Aggravated, Daniel hears the dial tone, tosses the phone on the floor and slowly turns to look at his blond friend who has a look of disappointment on her face.

Not one to ever let a moment like this pass him up, Daniel throws her back down on his couch. "Where were we?" he asks with a wicked smile and starting at her neck he slowly makes his way down to the treasure he desires, but just as he grasps her ankles to lift her legs up and over his shoulders he stops and looks up. "Hold on...did Bob just say I had to be at the airport in an hour?"

An hour later, frustrated and aggravated, Daniel climbs out of the backseat of a cab when the beautiful blond flight attendant grabs him, pulls him back inside and kisses him passionately.

"Mm," Daniel moans and pulling back slightly, he looks at her through heavy eyes. "Sorry about tonight, baby. Rain check?"

With a slight tilt of her head, she bites her lip and gives him a sexy smile. "Absolutely."

Reaching for her hand, he pulls it up to kiss it. "I can't wait."

"DANIEL!" Bob shouts and starts waving his hands to get Daniel's attention.

The blond looks behind him and sighs. "Just don't forget to call me when you get back."

"I won't."

"DANIEL!" Bob shouts again.

With a heavy sigh, Daniel backs out, grabs his bags and looks at the blond. "Gotta go, beautiful."

She sighs and as the cab pulls away she hangs out the window and blows Daniel a kiss.

"Who was that?" Bob asks running up behind him to hand Daniel his plane ticket.

"Flight attendant from First Class."

Bob laughs. "Only you."

Daniel smirks.

Turning to walk inside the airport, Bob hands Daniel his ticket.

"St. Lucia? Why are we flying to St. Lucia?"

Bob takes Daniel's bags and hands him a news brief from the Associated Press. "This is big, Daniel, really big and if I'm right this could be the story you've been waiting for."

Daniel reads the brief and looks at Bob. "Jesus, when did this happen?"

"Ten hours ago," Bob says as he leads Daniel to security. "At first, they thought it was a mass suicide, but then they found traces of Scopolamine at the beach house and the investigation changed."

Daniel's eyes widen. "Any sign of a struggle?"

Bob sighs. "Not sure, but Daniel, you and I both know what's been going on in the Caribbean over the last three months..."

Daniel closes his eyes and after clearing security they hurry to the gate and hand over their boarding passes.

"Daniel, there's more..."

Daniel takes his papers back and walks down the ramp to the plane. "What?"

"One of the dead volleyball players is the daughter of Arthur Chadwick."

Daniel's eyes widen. "The same Arthur Chadwick who owns Chadwick Broadcasting?"

"Yes, and that's not all...Chadwick's youngest daughter Arianna and her friend Marielle, who were also on the trip, have disappeared."

"What?"

"They're missing."

Daniel's eyes widen. "Any ransom demands?"

Bob steps on board. "No, not yet, but—

"But what?"

"I don't think we'll get one. I think Arianna and Marielle were abducted, and if I'm right we don't have much time before they disappear completely."

Daniel takes his seat. "What do you mean?"

"Daniel, these traffickers know what they're doing. They will get those girls out of St. Lucia immediately. Hell, I'd be surprised if they are still in the Caribbean. If we don't find a lead the trail will go cold and we will never find them."

Daniel sighs. "Jesus."

Bob tosses his bag in the overhead compartment and sits down next to Daniel. "When I first started investigating this network it was small, but it's grown from a pimp working the truck stops in Jersey to a full-fledged multi-billion-dollar business."

"Did you say billion?"

Bob nods. "These guys know what they are doing, they are making a lot of money at it and they will do anything to protect their investment," he says and leans in closer. "Daniel, they aren't going to stop unless we stop them."

Daniel turns to look at him. "What does that mean?"

Bob lets out a loud sigh. "The people behind this are well connected, smart and organized. It's not a local problem, it's a national problem that is now an international problem. They drive around cities scoping out runaways and people living on the streets. When they find someone, someone who could potentially make them a lot of money they move. Some of the victims are romanced and groomed, but others aren't so lucky."

"What do you mean 'romanced and groomed'?"

"The bad guys build trust, wait their victims out and when they think they're ready they introduce them to other girls who were once in their situation. Girls who will boast about the money they make, the things they have and the trips they take. They talk about living in sky rise apartments, going to college, dressing in fine clothes and brag about driving expensive cars. The victims buy into it; they practically volunteer for it, but this network in the Caribbean..." Bob mumbles and then sighs. "...it's different, aggressive and dangerous, nothing like the networks I'm talking about in the states."

Daniel exhales.

The engines roar to life and Bob leans over. "Prostitution is a multi-billion-dollar business, Daniel. There are networks all over the world, but these guys in the Caribbean are not like the other networks. They seem more organized, connected and tech savvy. They have a wealthy clientele of powerful men and women all over the world who value their privacy and they train their girls and boys. This network understands they are offering a service and they know their clientele will pay big for the perfect experience. They know how to play the game, they know just what to offer and how to offer it to attract the best candidates. They use their resources and most of their employees, for lack of a better term, come willingly, it's a business. If there is an abduction, they do it quickly and swiftly, no trace, but here is the scary part. This network doesn't just deal in human trafficking, they are just involved in drug trafficking and they are slowly taking over Europe, the Mediterranean and the Middle East."

Daniel shakes his head.

"This network prides itself on high-class service, nothing like the networks we are used to."

Daniel looks out the window as the plane taxi's down the runway.

"Daniel, this is the story you've been waiting for."

Daniel sighs. "Any witnesses?"

"One, but he isn't talking."

"Why not?"

"He refuses to talk to local law enforcement."

"Why?"

Bob turns to look at Daniel. "I don't know, but Chadwick thinks he'll talk to you."

Arriving in St. Lucia four and a half hours later Daniel is shocked to see all the media, but no sooner do they step off the plane and a black SUV pulls up alongside. Arthur Chadwick, a gray-haired man with dark rimmed glasses, gets out with an entourage of people surrounding him and makes his way toward Bob and Daniel.

"Bob!" Chadwick shouts and extends his hand.

After they shake, Bob turns to face Daniel and Arthur Chadwick extends his hand toward Daniel.

"Arthur," Daniel replies.

"Glad you're here," Chadwick says and clears his throat. "If we're done with the introductions, I'd like to get to the police station so you can speak with the eye witness. The clock is ticking."

Daniel nods. "Sure."

Once in the SUV Arthur turns to face Daniel. "I was in Hong Kong when I heard a team of volleyball players from Utah were found dead in their beachfront villa," he says his voice trailing off. "I immediately called my oldest daughter Annabelle, but got no answer. I tried to call my youngest daughter Arianna, but still no answer. I decided not to wait, ordered my pilot to get us to St. Lucia and that's when I got this message from the Associated Press... '*A girls' volleyball team from southern Utah was found dead in their beachfront villa at 2:10 this morning. Initial reports indicate a mass suicide; investigation is ongoing...*'."

Daniel glances over at Bob.

Arthur sighs. "Annabelle would not commit suicide."

Daniel nods and when the SUV pulls up in front of the police station he reaches for the door handle to get out when Arthur Chadwick stops him.

"Listen Daniel, I want to know what happened and I want to know now. Give the eyewitness whatever he wants; I have one daughter in the morgue and the other..." his voice cracks.

Daniel sees the look in his eyes and nods his head. "I'll do my best to get you some answers."

CHAPTER THREE

February 13, 1989

February in Washington D.C. is usually cold and snowy, but this year has been exceptionally bad. With record breaking snow fall, ice, and subzero temperatures the city has been paralyzed by one bad weather event after another.

Standing in his office at The Sun, looking out the window over Franklin Park, Daniel Donovan finds himself in a peculiar position. Normally, he would be spending his time chasing stories about corruption, political scandals, murder and intrigue; instead, he is writing about record snowfalls and insane winter storms.

Frustrated, Daniel pours himself a piping hot cup of coffee, sits down behind his desk and pulls out the file that has been burning a hole in his mind for seven months. An investigation that went cold way too fast, an investigation that has a personal connection, an investigation that still haunts him to this day.

Opening the file, he pulls out a picture of the twelve female college volleyball players and sighs before setting it down. Pulling out a second picture he studies Marielle Petrowski, a sixteen-year-old girl who loved animals and volunteered at the Stray Rescue Center. Turning his attention to the picture of Arianna Chadwick, he flashes back to her father's reaction in the black SUV on their way to the police station and rubs his face.

Leaning back in his chair, he rubs his jaw and glances over the pages upon pages of handwritten notes he took during the two-week investigation.

Per the eyewitness, the girls went out for dinner around eight, stayed to hang out with other teams and listen to music until midnight. Leaving the bar, they walked down to the beach to goof off, met some local guys and they all walked back to their beach house around 12:30. The eyewitness remembers it because he had just called his wife to tell her he was running late. Twenty minutes later, around 12:50, the eyewitness received a call from his dispatcher telling him there was a problem with a toilet in room 2204. He claims he got out of his truck and was walking toward the resort when he saw six men leave the beach house with two girls. He said the girls seemed dazed and unable to walk on their own.

Daniel leans forward with a loud sigh.

"Scopolamine was found at the scene," he mumbles and thinks about that. "Did they use it on the twelve volleyball players or the two missing girls?" he mumbles and looks back at the pictures. "Why wasn't there a fight?"

Daniel drops his head and thinks about that for a few seconds before he reaches for his last set of notes.

"The couple in the villa next door found them," he says and reaches for the notes he took when he interviewed the young couple. "When they came back from their walk on the beach they noticed all the lights on inside the girls' villa, heard the loud music and thought that was strange. They knew the girls were playing in the first round of the tournament in the morning so they stopped by to ask the girls to turn it down and that's when they discovered the gruesome scene."

Daniel looks off to the side.

"There was no sign of a rape, no sign of forced entry. The girls knew whoever was there with them. The only strange thing found at the scene was a powdery substance yet to be identified," he says to himself and closes his eyes to try to piece the puzzle together when he decides to look inside the first manila envelope he received from "Carl," an anonymous informant who started sending Daniel letters six weeks after the incident.

Reaching for it, he leans back in his chair and pulls out the handwritten note. "*Marielle and Arianna are not dead. They were sold to a man named Kristoff in France. They have no idea what is going on,*" he mumbles and reaches for the picture of two prostitutes walking the streets of Paris.

Daniel looks at the pictures of the two girls from St. Lucia and compares them to the picture of the two girls in Paris. "Is that you?" he asks out loud looking closer. "Is Bob right? Were you sold to the highest bidder? Is that what happened?" Daniel rubs his face and groans. "Who is Carl and how does he know so much?" he mutters and reaches inside the top right drawer of his desk to pull out six darts.

Walking across the room he tosses the first dart. A habit he got into in college when he was trying to sort out the details of the

Nixon vs. McGovern debacle. Tossing another dart, he hears something, turns to look but no one is there. Turning his attention back to the dartboard, he tosses another and then two more before he stops.

"The girls were drugged before they walked back to the villa," he mumbles. "Son of a bitch!" he shouts. "They were drugged at the bar!"

Excited with this new knowledge, he walks back to his desk when he notices another manila envelope on the seat of his chair, sees it is from Carl and looks up, his blood running cold.

With the hairs on the back of his neck standing straight up, he runs to the door of his office, looks out and to his surprise the office is empty and for some reason that freaks him out more than the envelope suddenly appearing on his chair.

Walking out of his office, Bob startles him and he jumps.

"Jesus, what is wrong with you?"

Daniel bends over to grab his knees. "Christ Bob, I thought you were someone else," he says and looks around. "Where is everyone?" he asks and walks back into his office.

Bob follows. "The mayor shut down the city, the National Guard has been called in to help with emergency snow removal of critical routes. The National Weather Service has issued a blizzard warning in effect until 3PM tomorrow evening. If they are right, we are looking at the chance of three feet of snow. I sent the staff to a hotel unless they live close."

Daniel nods with a loud sigh.

"What's wrong?"

Daniel shakes his head and points to the envelope on his chair. "Another letter from 'Carl'."

Bob's eyes widen. "How..."

Daniel pulls the darts from the dartboard. "I was throwing darts, thinking about Arianna Chadwick and Marielle Petrowski when I saw something out of the corner of my eye."

"Carl?"

Daniel rests his hands on his hips and shakes his head. "I was distracted I—

Bob's hands go up into his hair. "Jesus, Daniel, he was here?"

Daniel says nothing.

"What is wrong with you? What had you so engrossed that you wouldn't notice someone in your office?"

Daniel looks at him. "I think I figured out why there was no evidence of a struggle at the beach house. The girls were drugged before they got home. I think they were drugged at the bar, I think that's why the police found no evidence of a struggle, I think that's why Marielle and Arianna didn't fight back. They couldn't."

Bob stops. "Huh."

Putting on a pair of purple surgical gloves, Daniel reaches for the manila envelope, opens it and pours the contents into a plastic tub, the same plastic tub he uses every time he receives an anonymous letter like this.

Seeing a handwritten note, he reaches for it and holds it up in front of him.

"It's a list," he says and looks at Bob with a perplexed look on his face.

"What does it say?"

"One, investigate the Lara Stuart Modeling Agency and how they recruit. Two, investigate the connection between B&M Pharmaceuticals and S&S Healthcare. Three, find out which pharmaceutical companies are being considered to make and distribute the small pox and anthrax vaccine."

Daniel furrows his eyebrows and sets the note down, removes his purple gloves and sighs.

"What does that have to do with what happened in St. Lucia?"

"I don't know," Bob replies taking the note from Daniel.

Daniel walks around his desk and rubs his chin. "My mother worked for B&M Pharmaceuticals for twenty years, I know a lot about them, but I've never heard of S&S Healthcare."

Bob rubs his chin. "Lara Stuart owns the top modeling agency in the country, she is well known and well-respected. I wonder why he wants us to look into how she recruits," Bob mumbles and then he seems to remember something and wags his finger. "But, you know, I think B&M Pharmaceuticals was on the government's short list to make the small pox and anthrax vaccines," he says and jots something down on a piece of paper.

"Do you think it's all connected?"

Bob shrugs. "You want me to help?"

"I don't know, it's probably just another wild goose chase."

Bob looks at Daniel. "I'll see what I can find out."

CHAPTER FOUR

Arriving at The Sun the next morning, Daniel finds another envelope resting on his chair with his name on it.

Leaning out his door he shouts for Bob. "Bob, I got another envelope!"

Bob runs in just as Daniel is putting on his purple surgical gloves.

"Did you open it yet?"

Daniel shakes his head. "About to."

Bob moves to stand next to his desk and watches Daniel open the envelope and dump the contents into the tub.

"Jesus," Bob mumbles as more than a dozen pictures drop out.

Leaning forward to get a closer look Daniel reaches inside for the first picture. "It's a photo of a yacht named Glory Be."

Bob puts on a glove and reaches inside. "That's Lara Stuart." Bob mumbles and then he shakes his head. "I don't know who the man is sitting next to her, but that is definitely Lara Stuart," he says and tosses the picture back into the tub.

"Lara Stuart?" Daniel asks to make sure he heard Bob right and reaches into the tub to grab it. "The same Lara Stuart who owns the Lara Stuart Modeling Agency?"

Bob nods his head. "Yep, I met her at a gala in December," he mumbles distractedly and looks at the next picture. "I believe this picture is of Victor VonMeister and the next one is of Phillip Barnes, owners of B&M Pharmaceuticals," he mumbles and looks a little closer. "There is another man in the background, but I'm not sure who he is."

Daniel grabs the photos to get a better look. "What is going on? Are they all connected?"

"I don't know," Bob mumbles and then he holds up the last photo. "This last photo is interesting."

"Oh?"

Bob holds it up. "That's Congressman I.A. Hall," he says pointing to the man on the right. "Senator Robert Holmes is the man in the middle and Congressman Ira Weismann is on the left," he says and stares at it for a second or two. "It looks like they are on a fishing trip and if I'm not mistaken..." he mumbles and leans in closer. "I'm pretty sure that's Lara Stuart in the background with Phillip Barnes and Victor VonMeister."

Daniel immediately moves closer to get a better look. "Huh."

Bob leans back. "Looks like you have a mystery to solve."

Daniel's jaw clenches.

Bob removes his glove. "Look, Daniel, whoever this Carl guy is, he is giving you pieces to a puzzle, pointing you in a direction and it is up to you to figure it out."

Daniel sits down.

"There is something else I need to tell you," he says and hands Daniel another release from the Associated Press.

"Four more abductions?"

"This time in the Bahamas," Bob says and sits down on the corner of Daniel's desk. "Four friends from Westminster College. Two studying to be teachers, one was a business major and one was majoring in political science. They arrived Sunday, spent two days hanging out in the water and on the beach. Then they met these two guys who invited them to a beach party later that night. Julie Foster, the business major, called her parents to check in at 8:00 that evening, told them about the beach party, and said she would call in the morning to make sure her mother knew she was okay...she never called."

Daniel shakes head. "God."

"A body was found the next morning in a trashcan behind a gas station bound and gagged. There were traces of Scopolamine on her clothes and a powdery substance inside her nostrils. The victim was Julie Foster."

"No."

"I know, it's tragic, but here is the really interesting part. At first the police figured the powdery substance was Scopolamine but it turns out it was a drug called Maternix."

Daniel shakes his head.

"It's an infertility drug, it's not legal in the U.S. yet, but it is in the Caribbean and South America."

"Why would Julie Foster be taking an infertility drug and if she was why was she snorting it?"

Bob laughs. "She wasn't, Julie Foster ingested it. The powdery substance is known as Mama on the streets. It's Maternix in powder form, it's the new date rape drug."

Daniel looks up at Bob.

"The drug is still going through the FDA approval process in the states, but central and south America don't have the same strict guidelines so it's being manufactured in Colombia and sold worldwide."

"Is it an effective infertility drug?"

Bob shrugs. "I don't know. I've only heard of its illegal use."

Daniel turns to look at him.

Bob sits down. "Maternix comes in a vial. Inside is a freeze dried powdery pill that when mixed with saline becomes a powerful infertility drug, but if that freeze-dried pill is mixed into a drink it is more potent than Rohypnol."

"Jesus."

Bob leans forward. "But here is the insane part...if snorted it renders its female victims completely incapacitated and sends them into cardiac arrest."

"What?" Daniel asks with a laugh. "Are you serious?"

Bob nods and raises his hands. "I'm 100% serious."

"Jesus."

Bob stands. "Listen Daniel, Mama is becoming a public health crisis. According to my sources in Puerto Rico, female fatalities are skyrocketing."

"So, this Julie Foster goes to this party to meet up with these guys they met earlier in the day, one of them puts Mama in her drink and she passes out. I'm assuming she was raped."

Bob shrugs. "Still waiting on coroner's report."

"Then what? Does she wake up too early and they resort to spraying her with Scopolamine? If so, then when did she snort Mama?"

Bob looks at him. "We might never know," he says and walks toward the door. "Sounds like you have some work to do, let me know if you need some help and I'll see what I can find out about Lara Stuart."

Bob leaves and Daniel gets straight to work.

Diving into the investigation, he makes one call after another and by late afternoon he has three pages of notes, but then he receives a call that changes everything.

"Mr. Donovan, I understand you are investigating the body found in the dumpster behind a gas station in Nassau. I am a big fan of yours and I was at the gas station the night the body was found."

"Oh, did you see anything?"

"Yes. I am a cab driver in Nassau, I was taking a break to eat my dinner when I saw three men dump the girl's body."

Daniel frantically waves Bob into his office and Bob closes the door. "Okay, tell me what you know."

"First of all..." he mumbles. "I want to remain anonymous."

"Okay," Daniel mumbles and when Bob walks in he looks up. "You saw the men who dumped Julie Foster's body?"

"Yes."

"What time was that?"

"Around 3AM."

Daniel jots that down. "Did you recognize the three men who dumped her?"

"Yes."

Daniel's eyes widen.

"They are local drug dealers who work for Damian Santos Delabro."

Daniel stops and looks at Bob, who runs out of the office and when he returns he has his notepad.

"Do you know their names?"

The voice gets quiet for a second and Daniel can only hope he is coming to terms with what he needs to do.

"Look, Mr. Donovan, I have six kids, a wife I love and a good job. If they find out—

"No one will find out."

The man hesitates for several seconds and then he blurts out. "Esteban Ruiz, Luiz Sanchez, Emilio Reyes and another I do not know."

Daniel writes it all down. "Okay, got it. What about the other girls?"

The man's voice cracks. "They are gone, Mr. Donovan. They were taken."

Daniel looks up at Bob.

"I have to go," the man says, but then he stops. "...but there is one more thing I have to tell you before I do."

"Okay."

"Delabro is a dangerous man and if he finds out you are investigating him, he will kill you."

Daniel drops the phone down on his desk, looks at Bob and it's as if some unspoken word passes between them.

"I'm on it," Bob says and leaves quickly.

Seven hours later, Bob returns and finds Daniel staring at the white board next to his desk, a board that has all the pictures "Carl" sent as well as short notes.

"Figure anything out yet?" Bob asks.

"No," Daniel sighs and walks around his desk to sit back down. "I've made calls and no one will talk. There is a man I can't identify and now I'm wondering if this man is Delabro."

"Well, I'm not going to give you the silver bullet, but I do have information. The caller was right Esteban Ruiz, Luiz Sanchez, and Emilio Reyes are well-known drug dealers in the Bahamas as well as Miami. The Miami Dade police confirmed it and alluded to an on-going investigation about their involvement in trafficking drugs for Damian Santos Delabro."

"Do they have a picture of Delabro?"

"No. No one has ever gotten close enough to get a picture and he has never been filmed, either. Anyone who tries ends up six feet under or bait for the fishes."

"Great, so now what? It's like we have all these pieces to a puzzle and nothing fits."

Bob turns to look at Daniel. "Well, would it help you to know that we are not the only ones looking into Congressman Hall, Senator Holmes, and Congressman Weismann?"

Daniel turns to look at him and all the hairs on his neck and arms stand straight up. "What do you mean?"

"I have it on good authority that they are also being watched by the DOJ on allegations of corruption, racketeering, and solicitation."

"Jesus," Daniel mumbles and the hairs start to tingle.

Bob holds up a memo. "Oh, and I almost forgot...your dad called. He has been trying to get hold of you all day. Sounds like it might be important."

Daniel breaks his focus, looks at Bob, and then he nods his head to show he heard him. "Okay, thanks," he says and sets down the photo, removes his gloves, and makes the call.

"Hello."

"Ben, Daniel."

"Oh, hey, son. Listen, I'm taking your mother to New York City for her fiftieth birthday and we wanted to know if you'd like to join us."

Daniel smiles. "I wouldn't miss it for the world."

"Great, I'll send you our flight information."

"Okay, but I'm paying for it. The hotel, the festivities, the shows, and maybe even a Rangers game...what do you say?"

Ben smiles, Daniel can sense it. "I think that sounds amazing, son."

Daniel smiles. "Okay, I'll see you in two weeks. Give Mom a kiss for me."

"Will do."

Daniel ends the call and turns his focus back to the white board when his phone rings again.

"Donovan."

"Mr. Donovan, did you enjoy the pictures I sent you?"

Daniel looks up, sees it is nearly 12:18 in the afternoon and narrows his eyes. "Who is this?"

The voice on the other end sighs. "Did you receive the envelope?"

Daniel's eyes widen. "Yes," he says and reaches for a pen and a pad of paper. "Listen, Carl, maybe we should meet. I'm not sure what you want me to do with all this. What are you trying to tell me?"

"Everything is connected, Mr. Donovan. Figure it out."

Daniel sighs. "But I've looked into it and can't find a connection."

"You saw the photos, the people in them are very powerful. If they want to stop you, they will. It is up to you to find a way around them."

Daniel stops writing and looks at the pictures on his white board again.

"Mr. Donovan, which person in those photos has the most to lose? I want you to think about that when you watch the vote tomorrow morning. If I'm right the federal government will announce they have awarded a $274 million contract to B&M Pharmaceuticals to develop a small pox and anthrax vaccine and S&S Healthcare will be awarded the contract to distribute the vaccines."

Daniel looks over the pictures. "The vote isn't supposed to take place until nine o'clock tomorrow morning. How do you know that?"

"Who is on the congressional committee that is also in those photos? If you still can't figure it out, check out Dr. Reed Flynn from St. Louis. You might be surprised to learn that the good old Dr. Flynn's grandfather was one of the three original chemists who started B&M Pharmaceuticals. See if you can find out who owns his third of the company now."

"What do you mean, Flynn doesn't own his grandfather's company?"

The voice gets quiet for a second. "You'll understand only if you ask the right questions." the caller says and ends the call.

Bob walks by and sees the look on Daniel's face. "Hey, what's going on now?"

"That was Carl. We need to learn the history of B&M Pharmaceuticals. We need to find out everything we can about the original chemists who started the company and what happened to them." Daniel says scribbling down notes on his steno pad. "I also need the list of all the congressman on the Congressional Committee deciding the government contract to make and distribute the anthrax and small pox vaccines."

Bob's eyes widen, he nods his head and then he leaves.

Chapter Five

Working through the night, Bob walks into Daniel's office the next morning and finds him bent over his desk, face down, sound asleep.

"Hey," Bob says nudging Daniel so he'll wake up. "Hey, I have some news."

Daniel slowly opens his eyes, leans back and rubs his neck. "What?" he asks yawning loudly.

"Congressman Hall and Congressman Weismann are on the committee deciding the anthrax contracts."

Daniel's jaw drops. "Shit!" he shouts and gets up, reaches for the picture of Lara Stuart with the man he doesn't know. "We need to find out who this man is. Something tells me he is an important piece to this puzzle."

Bob takes the picture and looks at Daniel. "What are you going to do?"

"I'm going to find out everything I can about Dr. Reed Flynn, the three original chemists and how this is all connected."

"All right, let me know what you find out."

Sitting down at his desk, Daniel does a search of Dr. Reed Flynn and discovers he is a pediatric cardio thoracic surgeon at a children's hospital in St. Louis. Thinking for a second, he remembers his mother has a friend who works at the same hospital and decides to take a chance.

"Hello."

"Mrs. Burke, this is Daniel Beringer, I was wondering if you had a minute."

"Oh sure, Daniel. Does this have anything to do with your mother's fiftieth birthday?"

"No, ma'am, I'm calling to ask if you know a doctor Reed Flynn."

"Oh sure."

"Really," Daniel smiles. "How long you've known him?"

"Gee, I guess I've known Dr. Flynn since he was a resident."

25

"Is that a long time?"

"Oh yes, at least twenty years."

"Great," Daniel mutters and jots that down. "Do you know if Dr. Reed has any connection to B&M Pharmaceuticals?"

"Oh, uh..." she mumbles.

Daniel's spidey senses start to tingle.

"Why do you ask?"

"I'm investigating a story and his name came up."

"Are you investigating the story of little Christina Hall? I know the anniversary of her death is right around now. Does this have anything to do with the murder charges?"

Daniel's eyes widen. "Murder charges?"

Mrs. Burke gasps. "Oh, honey, it was an accident. Back then the residents worked more than a hundred hours per week, they lived at the hospital and rarely slept. He made a mistake, he never meant to kill her."

Daniel can't believe what he's hearing. "Reed killed Christina Hall? How?"

"Oh, Daniel, it was so sad. She was the youngest daughter of Congressman I.A. Hall and Beatrice Ayers Hall."

Daniel freezes. "Was he arrested?"

"Yes, but it was all very strange. One minute Congressman Hall is publicly condemning him, demanding his arrest, and then the charges were dropped."

Daniel squirms in his chair, his leg bouncing under his desk. "That's strange."

"Yes, it was. You know...you should write a story about Congressman Hall? I heard he might be running for the U.S. Senate."

Daniel is stuck in his thoughts for a second and then he snaps out of it. "I'll think about it. Right now, I need to know if there is a connection between Reed and B&M Pharmaceuticals."

"Oh."

"Why were the charges dropped?"

"I'm not really sure. We all assumed a plea bargain was reached."

The hair on Daniel's neck stands up. "What do you mean?"

She lets out a loud sigh. "You know, I don't know all that much about it, but I know someone who does...I think you should contact Lou Higgins at the Post. He was the investigative reporter who wrote the story."

"Story?"

"Oh yes, it was a big story here in St. Louis."

Daniel's ears perk up, and looking at the pictures once again he begins to see things differently. "Thanks Mrs. Burke, I'll talk to you soon."

"No problem, Daniel. Tell your mother I said 'hi',"

"Will do."

Daniel makes another call.

"Lou Higgins..."

"Mr. Higgins, my name is Daniel Donovan. I'm an investigative reporter for The Sun in D.C. and I'm investigating a man named Dr. Reed Flynn. I understand you wrote a story involving him and wanted to know if you had time to talk about it."

"Hold on...did you say you were Daniel Donovan from THE SUN?!"

"Yes." Daniel says and smiles.

"Well I'll be, what would you like to know?"

"I'm wondering if there is a connection between Congressman Hall and Dr. Flynn?"

"Which Dr. Flynn?" he asks.

"Is there another?"

"Oh yeah. Dr. Cathal Flynn...Reed's grandfather, the founder of B&M Pharmaceuticals."

Daniel eyes light up. "You're kidding?"

"Nope," Higgins mumbles and then he laughs. "Sounds like I just gave you an important piece of a puzzle."

"I think you may have," Daniel says and leans back in his chair. "Why don't you tell me everything you know about Reed and then you can tell me about Cathal."

Lou Higgins laughs. "Oh man, talk about a blast from the past...let's see....it was the early 70's..."

"I know a lot of time has passed, but I'll take whatever you can give me."

"Well, let me see...Dr. Flynn was in the final year of his surgical residency, working way more than he should have and he was exhausted. He had just worked four straight days and finally had a day off, but instead of going home he met some friends at a local bar for a drink. The combination of exhaustion and alcohol was a bad mix and on his way home he fell asleep at the wheel, the car jumped the curb, and plowed through a playground full of kids. A five-year-old, a seven-year-old and a three-year-old were hit, the three-year-old was caught under the car. She didn't survive."

"Oh, man!"

"Yeah, it was tragic, but what's worse is the victim's father saw it all and he did everything he could to save her."

"Oh?"

"The little girl was Christina Hall, the youngest daughter of Congressman Ian Angus Hall and heiress Beatrice Ayers-Hall."

The hairs on Daniel's neck start tingling.

"The congressman injured himself trying to save his daughter. He tried to crawl under the car to get her out, but couldn't get to her. By the time the fire department, police and paramedics arrived he had managed to jack the car up to get her out, but it was too late."

"Oh god."

"Hall was devastated. He turned all his anger toward Flynn. Wanted to make him pay and set out to destroy him. He wanted him in jail, he wanted his license and I'm pretty sure he wanted Flynn six feet under. Flynn was arrested, the incident was investigated and everyone expected the county prosecutor to call a grand jury, but Reed's father, Emmitt Flynn, hired the best attorney in the United States to defend his son and the next thing we knew Reed was released from jail and all the charges were dropped."

"What? You're kidding?"

"Emmitt Flynn died two days after Reed was released, a massive heart attack. I'm sure it was from all the stress," Higgins says and sighs.

"Why was Reed released?"

"No explanation was ever given. You have to understand...it was the 70's. Lots of corruption; especially in St. Louis, the good ole boy network had a way of manipulating everything and I.A. Hall was the Sinatra of the pack."

"Sounds like you have a theory, care to share?"

"I have my suspicions, but nothing concrete," Higgins murmurs. "I will say this...I'd bet money Hall found out about Reed's connection to Dr. Cathal Flynn..." he says, his voice rising.

Daniel takes out a new pad of paper. "Why would that matter?"

"Cathal was the founder of B&M Pharmaceuticals. A chemist from Belfast who stumbled upon one of the biggest chemical formulas of all time. A chemical that, if in the wrong hands, would had devastating effects and change the outcome of World War 1 and 2."

"Oh."

"As news spread of Cathal's finding, he became targeted by the Nazi's and the Russians. They wanted the formula and they were willing to do whatever it took to get their hands on it. Fearing for his family he contacted his good friend, Archibald Ayers, to help get his family out of Ireland and Archibald did. He brought them to the United States."

"How did Archibald and Cathal know each other?"

"They attended the same boarding school in Surrey; as a matter of fact, so did the Kelly brothers now that I think about it."

"Okay," Daniel mumbles not sure why this matters.

Higgins laughs. "Well, son, if you want to understand my conspiracy theory about the plea bargain you need to understand how Lake Forest came to be," he says.

Daniel rolls his eyes.

"Jedidiah, Padrig and Asher Kelly were from England. Their father, Lord Chief Justice Sir Robert Kelly, was a member of the Queen's counsel and in the mid-1800's the Queen ordered him to Belfast so he could preside over the courts and put an end to all the civil strife, but the problems in Belfast were too great and it was too dangerous for his family. Believing the only way to protect his sons was to get them out of Ireland, he sent them to a boarding school in Surrey where they met and became friends with Archibald Ayers and Cathal Flynn."

"Huh," Daniel mumbles and tosses his pen down on his desk.

"After boarding school the boys moved on to Cambridge and Oxford. Each finding his own success. Archibald went into finance and took on an apprenticeship in New York, Cathal became a chemist, Jedidah a surgeon, Asher a barrister, and Padrig a journalist, but the Kelly brothers were unsatisfied with life in England and longed to be part of the wide-open spaces they heard about in America."

"So, this is where you tell me they moved to St. Louis, right?"

"Yes, after their father died from a heart attack in 1872, they took their inheritance and invested it in several thousand acres of farm land in St. Louis County, west of the central corridor."

"Now this story is sounding familiar."

"The Kelly brothers loved St. Louis, they saw all the possibilities and when the city of St. Louis decided to divorce itself from St. Louis county they were given the opportunity of a lifetime."

"What does this have to do with Reed Flynn?"

"I'm getting there." Higgins says.

Daniel leans back in his chair with a smirk.

"The Kelly brothers met with nine others in the county, decided to donate a little over a hundred acres of land to create the new county seat of government, and in December of 1878 the new courthouse and jail opened in Lake Forest, but they didn't stop there. Two years later they sent for their friend Archibald Ayers to help plan and develop Lake Forest as the new county seat. By 1900, Lake Forest was the epicenter of government, commerce, medicine and industry. Leading the progress was a small chemical company named Flynn Chemical Company."

"Flynn Chemical Company? Never heard of it."

"Sure you have. Flynn Chemical Company was the parent company of BFM Pharmaceuticals."

"BFM Pharmaceuticals? Never heard of that either."

"You know it as B&M Pharmaceuticals."

"Huh, what did the 'F' stand for?"

"Flynn."

Now Daniel's interest is piqued.

"Cathal was very successful and the U.S. Government was his biggest client, but he had no interest in running the company so after his son graduated from George Washington University with a Master's degree in Finance he put him in charge. Emmitt's best friend was Archibald's son, Adrian Ayers, they went to college together."

"I know all about Adrian Ayers, he was the first billionaire in Missouri."

Higgins laughs. "Joining his father's Planning and Developing Firm in 1936, Adrian was determined to expand Lake Forest into a city that would rival that of New York and Chicago and with the help of his father and the Kelly brothers he did just that. Adrian introduced Emmitt and Cathal Flynn to two progressive thinking chemists, John Francis Barnes and Dimitri VonMeister, they created BFM Pharmaceuticals. With Emmitt's business sense and Barnes, VonMeister, and Flynn's brains, they built one of the most powerful Pharmaceutical companies in the world."

"I'm assuming John Francis Barnes is the father of Phillip Barnes and Dimitri VonMeister is the father of Victor VonMeister, right?"

"Right."

"So, Reed Flynn's family was worth a fortune."

"And very powerful."

"Why would Hall want Reed's money? He was married to Beatrice Ayers, isn't she worth billions?"

"Adrian cut Beatrice off when she married I.A., he didn't trust him and he was trying to protect her. I think I.A. wanted the shares in B&M Pharmaceutical's so he could amass his own wealth and use his power to ruin Adrian." Higgins says. "At the time of Emmitt's death his personal wealth was more than $300 million, but his third of BFM Pharmaceuticals was worth four times that amount. I think Hall found out Reed was Emmitt's sole heir. I think Hall wanted the shares and because Reed felt so guilty he signed it over as part of the plea bargain."

Daniel's jaw drops. "Jesus."

Suddenly the pieces of the puzzle start moving in front of Daniel's eyes. "Jesus, if that's true Congressman I.A. Hall committed fraud."

Higgins laughs. "Doesn't sound like you are investigating Flynn anymore."

"No, it doesn't...looks like I'm investigating Hall."

Higgins laughs.

"Did Hall ever go after Adrian Ayers?"

"He managed to get half of McCort Publishing, but that's all I know."

"Huh," Daniel mumbles.

"Let me know what you find on Hall. He's a slippery little sucker and I don't trust him any further than I could throw him. I've tried investigating him, but came up with nothing. It's as if the man didn't exist prior to arriving in the United States in 1948."

Daniel looks up, thinks about that for a second and nods his head. "Okay, thanks for the story and the information."

Sitting back in his chair, Daniel looks over his notes and as he does all the hairs on the back of his neck start tingling again. Staring out the window overlooking Franklin Square, he tries to connect more pieces of the puzzle when Bob barges in.

"Daniel! An announcement on the government contracts is about to be made."

Daniel reaches for the remote to turn on his television when his phone rings.

"Donovan," he says and turns his attention to the television to watch for the announcement.

The votes are cast and Bob slowly turns to look at Daniel. "Son of a bitch, it was rigged!"

Daniel nods his head, gets up to move I.A. Hall's picture to the middle of the white board and smirks. "Well, I'll be damned."

Bob joins him. "What does I.A. Hall have to do with the disappearance of Marielle Petrowski and Adrianna Chadwick?"

Bob's secretary knocks on the door. "Sir, Vice Admiral Paul Logan is on the phone for you."

Bob's jaw drops, Daniel's eyes widen.

"What the hell?" Bob mumbles and walks toward Daniel's door.

Daniel turns his attention back to his call. "Yes."

"Now do you believe me?"

CHAPTER SIX

Two hours later, Bob's secretary knocks on Daniel's door. "Daniel, Bob needs to see you in the main conference room."

Daniel nods, ends his call and leaves his office when he sees Arthur Chadwick, The Sun's lead counsel, and several others sitting around the conference room table.

Arthur stands to greet Daniel. "Hey, man, how are you?"

Daniel smirks. "I'm not sure, maybe you should tell me?"

Arthur puts his hands on his hips and with a smirk he shakes his head. "Looks like you've upset Homeland Security with your investigation."

Bob clears his throat. "Vice Admiral Paul Logan and U.S. Attorney Peyton Logan are requesting a meeting with you tomorrow morning. It seems you've been snooping around the same people they have under surveillance and they want you to stop."

The hairs on Daniels arms stand straight up and start tingling again. "Well, well."

Arthur Chadwick leans back in his chair. "They want to see you at the Pentagon first thing in the morning. They are sending a car."

Daniel smirks.

Bob looks at Daniel. "This is serious, Daniel."

"Jesus, what have I stumbled onto?"

Bob leans forward. "I don't know, but I have a feeling this might be the biggest story of your life."

Fourteen hours later Daniel is sitting in the back seat of a full sized black SUV.

Arriving at the Pentagon, a woman wearing a white military uniform escorts him inside and down a long corridor to a private conference room.

"Would you like something to drink?" she asks.

"Coffee..." he mumbles. "Black coffee would be great."

With a slight nod of her head, she turns and leaves.

A few moments later she returns with the coffee.

Trying to calm his nerves, Daniel takes a sip and thinks back to what Higgins told him about the sudden plea bargain. *Were the shares in B&M Pharmaceuticals worth letting your child's killer go free?*

Before he can think about that further, the door opens and two very large men wearing navy blue fatigues step in.

Daniel swallows. *I must be on to something big to cause all this.*

Stepping aside, Vice Admiral Logan walks into the room wearing his Navy whites and suddenly Daniel is in awe. Vice Admiral Logan is a big deal. One of the most powerful men in the country, and was recently put in charge of a special unit bridging the Department of Defense and Homeland Security. If his title doesn't intimidate you his looks will. He is tall, 6'3", with piercing green eyes and a short crew cut of white hair. He is tan, broad shouldered, fit and he exudes both power and testosterone in equal amounts.

Seeing the man in person, Daniel respects him immediately and can't help but be impressed. He has heard stories of Paul Logan, knows about his incredible missions in Vietnam and Korea while as a Navy Seal as well as his work with special ops. He is not someone Daniel wants to piss off, but he won't just roll over and give him what he wants either.

"Mr. Donovan," the Vice Admiral says and extends his hand, looks Daniel in the eye and freezes. "Or should I say Mr. Beringer?" he asks with this calmness about him that makes Daniel wonder what he knows about him.

Daniel's face falls. *Shit.* "Donovan is fine," Daniel says and they shake. Pulling his hand back he looks up at the Vice Admiral and tries to change the subject. "So, I understand congratulations are in order. I hear you have been appointed to a new division of Homeland Security."

Admiral Logan looks straight at him, says nothing, and then he extends his hand. "Have a seat," he says effectively avoiding the question. "The U.S. Attorney is running late, so we will begin without him," he says and sits down across from Daniel.

Watching Vice Admiral Logan, Daniel can't help but think about how powerful this man is, how many government secrets he must know and how many plots against the country, the president and top officials he has intercepted.

"I bet you intimidate even the most powerful heads of state."

The Vice Admiral looks at him and as if he triggered something the two men standing guard at the door move to stand guard on either side of him with their weapons at the ready and Daniel can't help but think that these men would lay down their lives for this man.

Removing his white hat, Admiral Logan sits back and seems to relax. "Tell me about this anonymous tip of yours, this man named 'Carl'."

Daniel smirks. "I'm not sure I want to do that, sir."

Vice Admiral Logan smiles. "I figured you'd say that," he says pushing a button on the remote in the middle of the table.

The woman who led Daniel to the conference room walks back in, hands the Vice Admiral several files and leaves.

"So, let's get right to the point," he mumbles and sets out the same pictures Daniel has already seen.

Daniel gasps. "How..."

Vice Admiral Logan looks at him. "Whoever is sending you this intelligence is also sending it to me and copying the U.S. Attorney as well."

Daniel's eyes widen.

"How did you confirm those contracts before they were announced?"

Daniel's eyes widen. "I have an informant."

"Alison Denney?"

Daniel's pulse jumps.

"Look, Daniel, you are poking around in my pond, disturbing my investigation and causing my people to get nervous and I don't like it."

"I'm sorry to hear that, but I'm not going to stop."

The Vice Admiral sighs. "I know and that's why I am going to do something I've never done. I'm going to tell you what I know and then you can tell me what you know," he says and leans back in his chair. "We'll call it a 'good faith' gesture."

Daniel doubts that, but listens anyway.

"First, to answer your question from earlier, you are right. I've been appointed to head a new division of Homeland Security. My job is to bridge the gap between Homeland Security, the Department of Defense, the CIA and the FBI."

Daniel's eyes widen.

"Its focus is to investigate, expose and eliminate scandals, corruption and illegal activities within our government, so you can understand why I'm interested as to why you are investigating two U.S. Congressman and one Senator."

Daniel drops his eyes.

Vice Admiral Paul Logan sees his reaction and leans forward. "So why don't you tell me why you are investigating Congressman Hall, Congressman Ira Weismann and Senator Robert Holmes."

Logan gets up to pour himself a cup of coffee and Daniel watches him walk around the conference table.

"To begin, I didn't know you were watching them. Their names keep popping up in my investigation. I think they may have something to do with this story I'm working on."

The Vice Admiral nods. "Like what?"

Daniel shrugs. "I'm not sure yet."

The Vice Admiral looks at him.

"Why are you watching them?"

The Vice Admiral returns to his seat, pushes a button on the remote and a picture of a beautiful red head pops up on the screen. "About fourteen years ago, a young college student named Sabrina Alphonso was brutally raped and left for dead in her sorority house after a visit from one of your Congressmen and his friends. She knew her attackers, turns out she was having an affair with him, but then he raped her and she didn't think she could go to the police."

Daniel's eyes widen. "Why?"

The Vice Admiral shakes his head in disbelief. "She didn't want to humiliate her family."

"Who—

"Sabrina decided to confront the man herself. She blamed him for what happened to her and decided to call him out in a very public place, but when he didn't balk at her outburst she did the only thing she could think of that would bring attention to him and opened a vein in front of him and half of Washington."

Daniel's eyes almost pop out of his head.

"She almost died," he says and sits back down.

"So, this incident with this college girl sparked your investigation?"

"Yes and no. It was her father, Carlos Alphonso, who did," the Admiral says watching Daniel like a hawk.

Daniel's eyes widen. "The same Carlos Alphonso whose family owns the largest shipping fleet in Spain?" Daniel asks sounding shocked. "Isn't he the son of Cristiano Alphonso?"

The Vice Admiral nods.

"Isn't Cristiano related to the King of Spain?"

"Yes, one of the King's brothers, but he is much more than that he is one of the most powerful politicians in the country and

36

he controls the shipping routes from the Mediterranean to the Atlantic."

"Did the Congressmen know she was related to him?"

Admiral Logan shakes his head. "No, we don't think so, but it was quickly turning into an international incident and that's when I was called in. I know Cristiano and Carlos; I have had dealings with them in the past and in order to bring calmness to the situation the higher ups put me in charge."

"What did you find?"

Vice Admiral Logan looks at him. "We found traces of Scopolamine in Sabrina's bedroom and we had never seen it before," he admits and then he shrugs. "To be honest, we didn't know much about it other than who produced it and controlled it," he says and slides a picture in front of Daniel.

Daniel leans over the table to look at it and gasps, points to the picture and looks up at the Vice Admiral.

Vice Admiral Logan narrows his eyes, his Spidey senses tingling. "Do you recognize him?"

Daniel swallows, considers his options, and then he nods his head. "First, you didn't receive all the same pictures from Carl. There are three missing. One with Congressman Hall, Congressman Ira Weismann, Senator Holmes, Victor VonMeister, Phillip Barnes, Lara Stuart and this man..." he says pointing to the picture.

"That man is Damian Santos Delabro."

Daniel gasps and his blood pressure just hit the roof. This story is starting to spin out of control.

Vice Admiral Logan is stoic, unmoving, and difficult to read. "The other two pictures, was Delabro in them?"

Daniel leans back in his chair. "Was Hall the man Sabrina was having an affair with?"

"Yes."

Daniel's eyes widen. *Jesus, I must be on to something big. He's answering my questions.* "Were Weismann and Holmes also involved in the rape?"

"Yes."

Daniel shakes his head. "There was a picture of Lara Stuart with Damian Santos Delabro on a smaller yacht with a man I didn't recognize, nor have we been able to identify. The last picture was of Phillip Barnes and Victor VonMeister with Hall, Stuart and Santos Delabro with the caption 'The Consortium' written on the back."

The Vice Admiral narrows his eyes and rubs his chin.

Daniel leans forward. "I received another envelope from 'Carl' yesterday morning with three bullet points...One to investigate how Lara Stuart recruits. Another about S&S Healthcare and B&M Pharmaceuticals. The last told me to identify the congressman on the Committee deciding the government contract for the anthrax and small pox vaccine."

Vice Admiral looks up at the two men and leans forward. "Is that what sparked your investigation into Hall?"

Daniel swallows. "No, it was an investigation into Dr. Reed Flynn that brought me to Hall."

Paul shows no emotion. "Who is Dr. Reed Flynn?"

Daniel looks at him and smiles. *He knows something the Vice Admiral doesn't know?* "Dr. Reed Flynn was a pediatric cardio thoracic surgical resident at a hospital in St. Louis when he fell asleep at the wheel. His car careened into a playground, injured two young children and killed one, three-year-old Christina Hall."

The Vice Admiral looks up.

Daniel sees his chance and pounces. "That's right, Congressman I.A. Hall's daughter," he says with an arrogant smirk. "According to my source, Hall wanted Flynn to pay for it, wanted him dead, but just as fast as he tried to discredit him it all came to abrupt end. My source believes Hall found out Reed Flynn was the sole heir of Cathal and Emmitt Flynn's fortunes, found out he just inherited 33 1/3% of BFM Pharmaceutical shares and..."

"You think Hall agreed to lesser charges in exchange of the shares?"

Daniel nods. "Beatrice Ayers Hall had all the money, she was the heiress to three fortunes. She was a descendant of the Kelly's who owned thousands of acres in St. Louis County as well as vast amounts of land out west and in Hawaii, her grandfather Gavin McCort owned one of the largest publishing houses in the United States, and her father is Adrian Ayers...I don't think I have to tell you about his net worth."

Vice Admiral Logan says nothing.

"Something tells me that Adrian Ayers saw through Hall, made sure to protect his daughter, and Hall was not privy to the kind of life he wanted so he took it from Reed Flynn. I think Hall is at the epicenter of my whole investigation...I just can't seem to connect all the dots."

The Vice Admiral says nothing.

Looking up at the Admiral, Daniel swallows. "You think I'm right, don't you?" he asks and leans forward. "You think it's all connected. Delabro, Stuart, the congressman and the senator, you think they are all connected just like I do?"

Admiral Logan looks at him.

Daniel realizes this is Logan's confirmation, he can't say it out loud, but the response is there.

Daniel looks up at the Admiral and sighs. "Look, my investigation started with the disappearance of Arianna Chadwick and Marielle Petrowski, it continued with the disappearance of three girls from Westminster College and every time I start to investigate a new lead the same names come up...I don't think it's a coincidence. I think Hall, Stuart, Delabro and the others are all connected and I think they know what happened to those girls."

Vice Admiral sits up straighter. "How can you be so sure?"

Daniel tries to make sense out of everything he knows out loud. "Hall is cocky and arrogant. Most of the country loves him because he is so charming, but I see through all that. I think Hall is devious, underhanded and I think he will do whatever it takes to get what he wants."

Vice Admiral leans back in his chair. "Sounds like you have personal experience with the man."

Daniel quickly tries to recover. "No, just the type," he says and watches the Vice Admiral closely. "I think Hall has been getting away with murder since he arrived in our country in 1948, not literally of course, but..." Daniel stops to think about that for a second and watches the Vice Admiral rub his chin. "What would Congressman Hall want with the head of a modeling agency, a drug lord, and two chemists?" he asks and leans back in his chair as he thinks about that.

"I don't know, Daniel, what do you think?"

Daniel leans forward abruptly and points to the picture of Hall. "You know what I think? I think Hall screwed up when he agreed to a plea bargain with Dr. Reed Flynn after killing his daughter."

Vice Admiral Logan smirks. "Why?"

The door opens and in walks U.S. Attorney Peyton Logan. "Sorry I'm late, what's this about Congressman Hall's daughter?" he asks and immediately sits down at the head of the table.

Daniel thinks he is seeing double, blinks twice, and then he tries to refocus. "Hold on...are you two..."

U.S. Attorney Peyton Logan nods his head and rolls his eyes. "Yes, we are identical twins, now let's get on with this."

Daniel looks at them again and smirks. "Well, I'll be damned..." he mumbles and then he looks at Peyton. "I spoke to a man named Higgins who writes for the Post in St. Louis. Dr. Reed Flynn was in his final year of his surgical residency when he made the biggest mistake of his life. After working more than a hundred hours that week, he left the hospital and instead of going home he joined some friends for a drink. On his way home, he fell asleep at the wheel, lost control of his car and plowed into a playground injuring two young girls, and killing three-year-old Christina Hall in the park across the street from the family home. Reed was arrested, a grand jury convened, but then the charges were dropped. Flynn never served any time and Hall left St. Louis. Higgins believes Flynn's shares in B&M Pharmaceuticals was the trade-off."

Vice Admiral Logan and U.S. Attorney Logan share a look.

Daniel leans forward. "What do you know about S&S Healthcare?"

Peyton looks down. "Nothing."

The Vice Admiral stares at Daniel.

Peyton reaches inside a file and pulls out a picture of a very tall red headed man with a thick beard. "Have you ever seen this man with Lara Stuart?"

Daniel looks and then he makes a strange sound. "I've never met her, but my editor has. If you give me a copy of the picture I will ask and get back to you."

Vice Admiral Logan pushes a button and Bob is escorted into the conference room.

"Peyton pushes the picture of a very tall red headed man with a thick beard in front of Bob. "Have you ever seen this man with Lara Stuart?"

Bob nods his head. "I believe so, but the man I met, Braden I believe, didn't have a beard."

The Vice Admiral pulls out another picture and lays it down in front of Bob. "How about this man?"

Daniel leans over to look at a picture of a tall man with black hair and a mole on his right cheek."

Bob nods. "I think so, yes, he was also with Lara. Who is he?"

Vice Admiral Logan sighs. "Anthony Leonetti."

Daniel's eyes widen as he reaches for the picture. "Did you say Leonetti?"

The Vice Admiral narrows his eyes and nods. "Yes, Anthony is the son of Tony Leonetti, a psychopath who murdered his father, his uncle and two of his brothers to get control of the family business in 1948."

Daniel swallows and flashes back to his birth certificate. *Maria Leonetti Donovan.*

"Hold on!" Daniel interjects splaying his hands out in front of him. "What was the name of the family business?"

Vice Admiral Logan looks directly at Daniel with a suspicious look on his face. "The name of the family business was Leonetti Trucking and Transport."

Daniel's heart starts racing; his breathing has changed. *Oh, my god, is my mother related to this family?* "What does Anthony have to do with Lara Stuart?"

"We don't know, we thought Anthony was dead."

"Dead?" Daniel asks his voice rising.

"Anthony disappeared in 1972." Peyton explains.

Vice Admiral Logan looks at Daniel. "I want you to do something for me," he says and glances over at Peyton as if seeking confirmation.

Daniel looks up at him. "What?"

"I know you went to college with Congressman Hall's son, Angus."

Daniel freezes, hardly able to breathe. *He knows!*

"I want you to get in touch with him and I want you to see what Angus knows about the shares, but more important than that we need to know if he knows anything about an event coming up in Miami."

"Event? What event?" Daniel mutters and looks at Bob.

Admiral Paul Logan stands. "If you find something out...call me," he says, turns and leaves with his brother following him out.

CHAPTER SEVEN

Leaving the Pentagon, Daniel's thoughts are scattered. He can't stop thinking about Angus and what happened between them in college, he can't stop thinking about the name Leonetti and what that name means to him and his mother, and he can't stop thinking about how much the Logan's know.

Angus and Daniel were close, they had an affair in college, it was sudden and it was different, but it was a sexual affair and when the Congressman found out about it he ordered Angus to resign. Angus protected Daniel and now he is about to violate their relationship to get information. Something about this feels wrong; they agreed to keep that part of their lives a secret, but now he risks exposing them both.

Arriving back at The Sun, Bob orders a team of junior investigators into Daniel's office and tells them they are working for Daniel now. Leaving, Daniel takes over.

"Your first assignment is to find out everything you can about the Leonetti family, Leonetti Trucking and Transport and to learn everything you can about each family member. Second, I need you to find out everything you can about S&S Healthcare. Who owns it, where it's headquartered, and how long they've been in business," he says and his phone rings.

Reaching for his phone, he holds up his finger and immediately answers it. "Donovan."

"Do you believe me now?"

Daniel sighs. "Look, I have investigated everything you gave me, but I'm still not sure what I'm looking for?"

The voice on the other line is silent. "Don't you think it's strange that a government contract was issued to a man and woman suspected of being involved in a Human Trafficking ring for sexual exploitation," the caller says. "Contact Emma Brown's family, she's been missing since April, ask them what happened," he adds and the line goes dead.

"Shit!" Daniel shouts. "I knew it! I knew Logan wasn't telling me everything. I knew there had to be more to the story about why they were investigating the congressman. Shit, shit, shit, shit, shit!" Daniel shouts again and starts pacing the room. "I'm not sure why, but see what you can find on the disappearance of a girl named Emma Brown, she disappeared last April."

The team leaves and two hours later Elise, one of the junior investigators walks into his office.

"We think we have something."

Asking Daniel to meet her and the team in the conference room, two investigators from the Criminal Crimes Division join them, but before Daniel can leave his office his phone rings.

"Donovan."

"Hey man," a familiar voice says.

Daniel looks up. "Angus?" he asks, stunned and stupefied to hear his voice. "Thanks for calling me back, man!" he shouts trying not to reveal how nervous he is.

Angus laughs. "Of course, what's going on?"

Daniel stops for a second, thinks about Vice Admiral Logan and shoves his hand into his hair. "I...uh."

Angus laughs again. "Sounds like you are working on a story. What's got you so rattled?"

Daniel drops his hand and sighs. "Oh, man, it's...I'm frustrated."

"Sounds like it." Angus says with a smirk. "Hey, listen, I was summoned to D.C. by my father, but he had to leave suddenly. Any chance we could have dinner tonight?"

Daniel walks over to the large picture window and swallows. "Sure," he says sounding a bit nervous. "So how is the old man?"

Angus smirks. "I have no idea. We haven't talked much since..." he exhales. "I arrived this morning, he met me at his Brownstone and then something came up and he left."

"What do you mean?"

Angus sighs. "I don't know. He mentioned something about Sault Ste. Marie."

Daniel jerks his head back and makes a sour face. *Why does that sound so familiar?* "What's in Sault Ste. Marie?"

Angus is quiet for a moment. "I have no idea," he says and laughs out loud. "But one thing is for sure...whatever it was it must be important because he left without a bag."

"Hmm, sounds intriguing."

"Only if I'm Daniel Donovan."

Daniel laughs.

Angus gets quiet. "So how about dinner? There is something I need to tell you and I think it should be in person."

"Sure."

"Okay, I'll meet you at O'Shea's Pub at seven."

Michael D'Angelo, lead reporter for the Criminal Crimes Division of The Sun walks into Daniel's office. "So, I understand you want to know about the Leonetti's?"

Daniel nods his head and motions for D'Angelo to follow him to the conference room, takes a seat and the next thing he knows Bob walks in with Arthur Chadwick to join them.

"Well ..." D'Angelo mumbles and nods to his assistant who places eight large boxes on the table. Leaning forward he opens the first box marked Salvatore and Angelo, pulls out a dozen pictures, and tosses them on the table. "Salvatore and Angelo Leonetti came to the United States from Palermo in the early 1900's, and settled in Chicago to start an Ice business," he says and hands out another picture. "A few years later they expanded their business into Leonetti Trucking and Transport."

The assistant plops down more pictures. "During the early 1920's the business was doing so well they opened a second location in St. Louis."

"Did he stay in Chicago or move to St. Louis."

"He sent his brother to St. Louis and stayed in Chicago. You have to understand...by the time they opened the second location Sal had four teenage sons, a pregnant wife and he had established himself in Chicago. The Leonetti's were a big deal."

Daniel's smirks.

"Everything was going really well for the Leonetti's until his wife died giving birth to their first daughter. Sal was devastated."

Daniel looks at all their pictures and sighs. "What was her name?"

"Ava."

"How many kids they have?"

"Five. Sal, Jr., Guitano, Tony, Lucca and Gianna."

"Did Sal ever marry again?"

Everyone looks at Daniel.

He sees their reaction and drops his eyes. "I just want to hear the whole story."

D'Angelo shrugs. "Yes. Big Sal put Sal Jr., in charge of Chicago and took baby Gianna back to Palermo. I guess he needed his family's help," he says and tosses down more pictures of Sal and baby Gianna.

"What happened to the business in Chicago?"

"It grew! Sal Jr. ran the business better than his father. He saw the success of the docks in St. Louis, built docks on Lake

Michigan, and opened a third transport office in Quebec. The company was doing well and Leonetti Trucking and Transport grew like crazy. Sal Jr. took the company from delivering goods and services to the Midwest and the north to the east and the south. The business wasn't the problem. It was Tony Leonetti who was the problem. He had gotten mixed up with some bad people, he was doing some bad things and he was in and out of jail because of it. At one point, it got so bad, Angelo had to come back to Chicago because Tony was running drugs to New York with Leonetti trucks. When Salvatore returned a year later the business was in great shape, but his family wasn't. Tony was out of control and Lucca was following in his footsteps."

"Tony's the one who killed his father and brothers, right?"

D'Angelo nods.

"Did Sal take over when he got back?"

"Not really. When Sal returned, he had a new wife, but more than that he had a pregnant new wife who was only fifteen."

Everyone's jaw drops.

Michael D'Angelo laughs. "Francesca Andolini was the only daughter of Emilio Andolini, an Italian shipping magnate who wasn't as big as the Greeks, but just as powerful as the Spaniards. Their marriage was a business deal. Emilio didn't trust Mussolini and his fascist regime, so he paid Salvatore to get Francesca out of Italy and signed over the Andolini Shipping Company to Francesca as an act of good faith."

Daniel takes the picture and his eyes almost pop out of his head. "Did you say her name was Francesca?"

D'Angelo nods his head. "Yes."

Daniel takes a closer look. "You say she was fifteen when she married Sal?"

D'Angelo nods. "Yes, they married in February of 1922."

Daniel looks up at D'Angelo. "How did Salvatore's sons react to him bringing home a wife who was younger than them? Did it cause tension?"

D'Angelo continues. "I don't think so," he says with a chuckle. "They saw it as a business merger. With Andolini Shipping, their business was about to become the largest shipping and transport business in the United States."

Daniel leans forward to look at more pictures of Francesca and seems out of sorts. "So, did Angelo return to St. Louis after Sal got back?"

"No, Francesca didn't like Chicago, she had family in St. Louis, so Sal left Sal Jr. in charge of Chicago, moved Guitano to

Quebec and he moved the headquarters to St. Louis. Angelo joined him."

"Why didn't Francesca like Chicago?"

Michael holds up his finger. "Tony."

Daniel slowly turns to look at him.

"Tony was a psychopath and when he got involved with the mob it got worse."

The assistant pipes in. "Big Sal gave Tony an ultimatum, Tony either cleaned up his act, or he was cut off...Tony chose wrong. Sal cut him off and forbid the family to have anything to do with him."

Daniel swallows. "What happened?"

"Tony moved to New York, started working for the head of the New York crime family as an enforcer, got the head of the New York family's daughter pregnant, and the old man told him he either marry the girl or he could swim with the fishes. Tony married the girl, but she was just as crazy as he was and after giving birth she managed to get her hands on a scalpel, opened a vein and when they found her two hours later she was dead."

"Jesus," Daniel scoffs.

"Tony left with the child, returned to Chicago and Sal Jr. took pity on him, put him in charge of the docks and Tony seemed to be straightening out his act until 1950 when Tony got fed up with being a worker and decided he wanted his part of the Leonetti pie. The only problem was his family didn't agree."

Daniel looks up.

"Tony befriended a dockhand, convinced the guy to help him, agreed to pay him well and started putting a plan together to seek his revenge."

"Revenge?"

"Francesca wanted nothing to do with Tony and Tony hated Francesca, but he really resented her son Michael. Michael grew up in the wealthy community of Knights Meadow in Lake Forest, he attended all the finest schools, dressed in nice clothes, played golf and tennis, and he had movie star good looks. Michael had it all, but then he knocked up some debutante, he was fifteen at the time, and the debutante was sixteen. Her parents hit the roof, sent her away to have the child, forced her to put it up from adoption and then Francesca found out."

Daniel looks up.

"No one knows what happened, but the order of nuns received a sizeable donation and Francesca returned to Lake Forest with Michael's child."

"What is the child's name?" Daniel asks.

Michael D'Angelo looks down at his notes. "Maria Francesca Leonetti."

Daniel's jaw drops. "When was the child born?"

The assistant looks again. "June 16, 1938?"

Daniel reaches up with both hands to rub his face. "Oh, my god."

Everyone turns to look at him.

Daniel looks up. "So, are the stories true? Did Tony kill Sal and his brothers?"

The assistant nods his head. "Yes. He murdered all three of his brothers, tossed their bodies into Lake Michigan and assassinated Sal on the tarmac as he walked off the plane."

"What was in the truck?"

"Two bombs. They detonated as Angelo opened the back of the truck to see what was inside."

"Jesus," Daniel mumbles.

"The Lake Forest police arrived at the birthday party, told Francesca what happened and fearing the family was under attack ordered everyone to leave, but there was a problem. One of Maria's friends was missing and no one could find Anthony. Michael ordered his men to start looking for them and ran off with the man who brought Anthony to join the search. Moments later the stables at Knights Meadow went up in flames, Anthony disappeared and the body of a ten-year-old girl was recovered in the rubble the next day."

"Christ!" Daniel shouts and reaches for a picture of Anthony Leonetti. "What happened to Tony?"

"He was arrested and spent the rest of his life in jail as far as we know."

"What about Anthony?"

"He showed up two days later, Francesca agreed to take him in after Tony was arrested and charged, but that didn't last long. He was as crazy as his father and Francesca was forced to send him to a mental facility to try and straighten him out. It didn't work. He walked out the day he turned eighteen and disappeared. Everyone figured he was dead."

Daniel exhales. "Any idea who the man was Tony befriended?"

They both smirk. "We don't know for sure, but Ian Angus Hall worked on the docks in Chicago for Leonetti Trucking and Transport in 1948 and two weeks after the murders he was promoted to Vice President of Marketing, moved to the headquarters in St. Louis and was given a house and a new car. Sounds suspicious, doesn't it?"

Everyone's jaw drops.

Bob stands. "What does this have to do with your investigation?"

D'Angelo looks at Daniel. "The man in the picture you sent me, the man with Lara Stuart? It's Anthony Leonetti."

CHAPTER EIGHT

Arriving at O'Shea's Pub to meet up with his old friend, Daniel is still in shock, still trying to connect all the dots.

"Daniel!" Angus shouts and when the two friends see each other they both explode into big smiles.

With a quick hug and a slap on the back the old friends seem genuinely happy to see one another, but the happy reunion doesn't last long. Grabbing a couple of beers from the bar, they step off to the side to wait for a table when two women accost Daniel.

"Are you Daniel Donovan?" the blond with large breasts asks.

Daniel smiles. "Yes, I am and you are?"

"Jennifer," she says and smiles a sexy little smile before turning toward her friend. "And this is my friend Eve."

Daniel quickly nods his head. "It's nice to meet you."

Jennifer leans in closer, her lips almost touching his ear. "Do you have plans this evening?" she asks and slides her number inside the pocket of his jeans.

Daniel looks down at her, but before he can answer the hostess calls his name and distracts him.

Waving his hand toward the hostess he looks down at the buxom blond and smiles. "Maybe some other time, beautiful, gotta go," he says and kisses her cheek before stepping back to follow Angus to their table.

Angus shakes his head. "Still the same old Daniel I see."

Daniel smirks, follows the hostess to a table tucked away in the corner of the room and sits down, and after taking the menu from the hostess he watches her leave.

Angus clears his throat. "You know, I never realized you were so much like my father."

Daniel immediately looks up. "What?"

Angus laughs. "My father is quite the womanizer, just like you."

Daniel gives Angus a look and sets down his menu.

Angus smirks.

"So, what is going on? What did you want to tell me?"

49

Angus looks at Daniel. "I'm getting married."

Daniel stops drinking. "What?"

Angus drops his head and blushes. "You aren't the only one who has moved on."

Daniel sets down his drink. "Angus—

A waiter arrives. "Hi there, may I take your order?" the tall, dark haired man asks as he stares at Angus.

Angus smiles and orders the fresh Atlantic salmon with saffron risotto and asparagus.

"Salad?" the waiter asks and licks his lips, obviously flirting with Angus.

Angus nods his head. "Yes, thank you."

Daniel can't help but laugh.

The waiter turns to face Daniel. "And you?"

"Porterhouse, loaded baked potato and I think I'll go for one of those Caesar salads."

The waiter nods his head and starts to leave when Angus stops him, smiles and asks him to bring a bottle of his best merlot.

Daniel smirks and when the waiter leaves he narrows his eyes. "Still the same Angus I see."

Angus looks at him and smiles. "What can I say?"

"So, how did this happen?"

Angus nods. "After Dad found out about my affair with one of my students in college," he says with a slight glance in Daniel's direction. "...he insisted I take a job at McCort Hall Publishing and introduced me to Harriet Sanders."

"Hold on, Harriet Sanders of Sanders Tobacco?"

Angus nods. "Sampson's only daughter."

"And devout Democrats who love your father, right?"

Angus raises his beer. "It is an election year and he wants that senate seat."

Daniel exhales. "Now things are making sense."

Angus smirks. "We can't all be Daniel Donovan."

"What does that mean?"

"Oh, come on!" Angus shouts. "Daniel, you've got it all. You're smart, you've got a great job, you're great looking, girls won't stop throwing themselves at you...every guy wants to be you."

Daniel drops his eyes.

Angus laughs. "It's like being with a rock star or a movie star. You seem to command attention wherever you go," he says, drops his head and shakes it. "I'm in awe of you."

Daniel sighs and finishes his beer just as the waiter arrives with their salads, two glasses and a bottle of merlot.

Angus changes the subject. "Tell me about this story that has you so out of sorts."

Daniel laughs. "Is this a conversation starter or are you genuinely curious."

"Genuinely curious..."

Daniel smirks and pours the wine. "Before I tell you, answer a question for me. Why are you getting married?"

Angus sighs. "My father can't have a gay son if he wants the senate nomination."

Daniel's eyes widen.

Angus looks away. "Harriet is nice, dull and ugly, but nice."

"But..."

Angus holds up his hand. "Let's change the subject...I want to know about the story."

Daniel looks at him and sighs. "It all started back in July when twelve college volleyball players were found dead at their beachfront villa..."

Angus narrows his eyes.

"They were there for a beach volleyball tournament, went out to dinner one night, met some locals who I believe drugged them and something went wrong. The coroner said they all died from cardiac arrest."

"Jesus."

Daniel looks at him. "That's not all. There were two sixteen-year-old girls on the trip, Arianna Chadwick and Marielle Petrowski, who disappeared out of thin air."

Angus holds up his finger. "Hold on, did you say Chadwick?" Angus asks. "Any relation to Ar—

Daniel nods. "His youngest daughter."

"Oh, my god, I heard about this...Dad told me about this. He was really upset about it."

Daniel's eyes widen. "Huh, I wonder why. Arthur doesn't know your father."

Angus shrugs. "I don't know. Do you have any idea what happened?"

"I think they were abducted."

Angus looks up. "Any witnesses?"

Daniel nods. "One, he saw the girls being led away by six men."

Angus swallows. "Shit."

Daniel clears his throat.

Angus looks at him.

Daniel finishes his salad and pushes his plate away. "There is this guy named Carl. He's been sending me handwritten notes and pictures since November."

Angus looks up.

Daniel shrugs. "Whoever Carl is, he seems to know what happened and he wants me to blow the whistle on it. He's been feeding me information, helping me connect the dots, but I'm still not sure what he wants me to find."

"What has he sent you?"

The waiter arrives with their meals, smiles at Angus and sets it all down.

Daniel laughs, shakes his head and as soon as the waiter leaves he leans forward. "Does Harriet know you're gay?"

Angus smiles. "Yes."

"She does?"

"She doesn't care," Angus says with a shrug. "We have a little arrangement. I agree to give her two children; she gives me the freedom to be who I want to be."

Daniel looks at him. "And all the while your Dad thinks..."

Angus nods. "He thinks I am doing exactly what he wants."

Daniel is speechless.

"So, what has this informant 'Carl' sent you?"

Daniel drops his eyes and tries to avoid the question.

Angus sees his reaction and sighs. "This has something to do with my father, doesn't it?"

"I don't know yet, but it's leaning in that direction."

Angus leans back. "Tell me what is going on."

Daniel looks at him, thinks about it and decides to go for it. "What do you know about B&M Pharmaceuticals?"

Angus narrows his eyes. "A lot; I'm a shareholder, why?"

Daniel stops eating. "You're a shareholder?"

"Yeah, I inherited 331/3 shares on my twenty-fifth birthday, why?"

Daniel looks around. "What do you mean you inherited them?"

Angus shrugs and takes another bite of his salmon. "I don't know. I think it came from Adrian Ayers, Beatrice's father. He always treated me the same as the others, he never made me feel like I wasn't family, I just assumed..."

Daniel leans forward. "Angus, the shares didn't come from Adrian Ayers. They came from your Reed Flynn or rather...your father."

"What?" Angus asks looking shocked.

Daniel's jaw clenches. "Another piece of the puzzle."

Angus looks at him with a perplexed look on his face. "Puzzle, what puzzle?"

Daniel tells him about Dr. Reed Flynn, Cathal Flynn, the Kelly brothers and Archibald Ayers before he tells him he knows Reed killed Christina, Angus' half-sister, and what he believes happened between I.A. and Reed as part of some under the table plea bargain. Angus is stunned.

"Man, I remember when Christina was killed. It was my first year of college and I'll never forget the phone call from Beatrice asking me to come home," he mumbles and looks away. "You think my father found out about Reed's inheritance and used it to blackmail him?"

Daniel nods.

Angus finishes his last bite and tosses his napkin down on the table, holds up his finger to call the waiter over and orders a scotch.

"Angus."

Angus looks at Daniel. "Listen, Daniel, I don't doubt anything you are saying to me and I'm pretty sure you're right about my father, but if you are thinking that's enough to bring him down..."

"Oh, I don't, but there's more."

The waiter arrives with Angus' scotch and sets it down, smiles at him and then he leaves. Daniel reaches into the inside pocket of his blazer, pulls out the pictures and sets them down on the table.

"What is this?"

"Pictures Carl sent me, says they are all connected."

Angus nods and reaches for one. "Well, some are."

Daniel's eyes widen. "What do you mean?"

"Lara Stuart is a good friend of my father's, Senator Robert Holmes and Congressman Ira Weismann are, too. They've known each other for years; as a matter of fact, they all get together four times a year and meet up in the Caribbean or something like that. I've been invited to go on the next trip. Dad has never extended an invitation to anyone of us until now."

Daniel narrows his eyes.

"I was going to invite you along, it's this weekend."

Daniel's eyes almost bug out of his head and he immediately leans closer. "How can you take me along when your Dad knows about us?"

"He doesn't know I had an affair with you. He only knows it was a college student of mine when I was teaching at the university."

Daniel looks around to make sure no one heard that and sighs. "How can you be sure?"

Angus looks at him. "First, your name in college was Daniel Beringer. You didn't change to Daniel Donovan until after you graduated. Second, I covered my tracks. My father thinks the guy was an English major."

Daniel leans back and blows out a loud breath of air. "All right, one more question. Do you know anything about S&S Healthcare?"

Angus thinks for a second. "Sounds familiar, I remember reading something about it before our last shareholder's meeting," he says and wags his finger as if trying to remember something and suddenly looks up at Daniel. "I think it's based out of Miami."

Daniel takes in a sudden breath air. "You sure?"

Angus shrugs. "No, but I'll look through my notes. What else did this Carl guy say?"

Daniel shakes his head, considers his next move and sighs. "Carl knew the government was going to award B&M Pharmaceuticals the $274 Million contract to make both the anthrax and small pox vaccine and he knew the distribution contract would be issued to S&S Healthcare."

Angus' eyes widen. "Shit, my father was part of the Congressional committee deciding the contracts."

Daniel slowly nods his head.

Angus looks shocked. "Jesus, do you know what this means?"

Daniel nods. "That's not all..." he says and pulls out the pictures of Arianna Chadwick and Marielle Petrowski while in St. Lucia and the one Carl sent him of the two girls in Paris.

"What's this?"

"Pictures of Arianna and Marielle in St. Lucia and recently in Paris."

Angus' eyes widen. "You think my father had something to do with that, too?"

Daniel shrugs. "I don't know," he admits and puts down two more pictures.

Angus looks them over and nods his head. "The red headed man is my father's head of security. His name is Braden Stuart I think he is Lara's son. The other guy is Anthony, but I don't know his last name. Dad keeps him away from the family."

Daniel can't believe what he's hearing. "Angus..."

Angus raises his hand to stop him. "Don't. I know the kind of man my father is. He is out for one thing...himself. Dad never cared about anyone. He's a user and I think he is a dangerous guy. I'm not surprised about any of this."

Daniel pulls out one more picture, the picture of Sabrina Alphonso and sets it down. "Have you ever seen this woman?"

Angus stares at the picture for a long time and then he looks at Daniel. "I think so...this woman is a lot younger, but I think that's Sadie. A woman my father has a relationship with."

Daniel takes the picture back. "Still?"

Angus nods. "I don't know for sure, but I think so," he says. "Why?"

Daniel looks at him and sighs out loud. "This girl was brutally raped in college and left for dead. The Department of Justice and Admiral Paul Logan believe your father was involved."

Angus' eyes flash up to meet Daniel's. "Jesus..." he mumbles and then he leans back and releases a large breath of air. My father has a large appetite for sex, the younger the better. I wouldn't be surprised to learn he was involved. He is very controlling," he confesses looking down. "I remember some of the parties he had when we first moved to St. Louis. Women were constantly coming and going. Dad liked it often and he liked it rough. I never understood why Beatrice married him."

"Angus, what if I'm right."

The waiter arrives to clear the table and Angus orders another scotch.

Daniel holds up his finger. "Make that two."

The waiter nods his head and leaves, disappointed that Angus doesn't acknowledge him.

Angus looks at Daniel. "I think you need to do what you have to do, but I do have one request..."

Daniel nods.

"Let me know before the story breaks."

Daniel looks at Angus.

"Listen, Daniel, I know the kind of man my father is and nothing you've showed me or told me surprises me, but I also feel like I need to warn you. I.A. is dangerous. There is a monster buried deep inside him and he will do anything to get what he wants so be careful."

"Okay, but now I have one more question..." Daniel says and shows Angus the picture of Lara Stuart and Damian Santos Delabro again. "Do you know the man in this picture?"

Angus shrugs. "I don't know his name, but I've seen pictures of him with Dad and Lara before. I'm pretty sure they do business together."

The hostess walks up to the table. "Excuse me, Mr. Donovan, but you have a call at the hostess station."

Daniel looks surprised. "I do?"

"Yes, would you like to take it or would you rather me take a message?"

"I'll take it says and scoots out of the booth. "Donovan."

"Glory Be is docked in Miami." the caller mumbles and hangs up.

Angus joins him. "Is everything alright?"

Daniel looks at him. "Where is this trip you are taking with your father?"

"Miami."

"Shit."

"What?"

"I don't know, but something tells me I'm about to break the biggest story of my life."

CHAPTER NINE

February 16, 1989

Sitting in his oversized leather chair, hunched over with this head on his desk, Daniel is sound asleep when Bob walks in.

"Daniel!" Bob shouts sounding irritated and excited all at once. .

Daniel slowly raises his head. "Jesus, what?"

"Enough sleeping, your phone has been ringing off the hook, the switchboard has taken several messages. I placed them on your desk," he says and starts for the door. "Get it together; I want to speak to you in twenty minutes."

Daniel looks up at him and nods his head. "Fine."

Flipping through the messages he sees three without a name, each one recorded thirty minutes apart, and a dozen or so from Angus demanding Daniel call him immediately, but the last two are from his mother and being the good son he is he calls her first.

"Mom!"

"Hi, honey, where have you been?"

Hearing her voice settles him down immediately and he rubs his face. "I've been working."

"Big story?"

"Yeah," he says and yawns. "Mom, do you have a minute?"

"Sure," she says and then she giggles. "Mary Beth said you called her the other night, she was so surprised to hear from you, but then she said you asked about Dr. Reed Flynn, is everything alright?"

He sits up straighter. "That's sort of what I want to talk to you about."

"Oh."

"This case I'm working on has ties to St. Louis and I was wondering if I could ask you some questions."

She hesitates for a moment, something she does when she gets nervous.

"Mom, are you related to Salvatore and Francesca Leonetti?"

She gasps, he can hear it even though it is subtle.

"Mom, I need to know."

"Why?"

"There is a man named Anthony Leonetti who I'm investigating and—

"Oh god, oh god, Daniel don't go near him, stay away from him! Oh, god, oh god."

He sits up, wide awake and full of concern. "Mom, I haven't met him, but I am investigating him and I need to know who he is."

"Oh god, Daniel. Oh, god."

"Mom, calm down and talk to me. Are you related to Salvatore and Francesca Leonetti?"

She starts sobbing. "Yes," she whispers. "I never wanted you to know, but yes."

"Mom," he says a little louder. "Why do you keep things from me? First, my biological father, now this, what are you doing?"

She starts to sob and after giving her a few minutes to calm down he gets quieter and talks nicer.

"Mom, talk to me."

She takes a deep breath and exhales. "Salvatore Leonetti was my grandfather, Francesca is my grandmother, but it is a long story and—

"Tell me."

She takes another deep breath and exhales. "Oh Daniel," she says with a loud sigh. "It all started when Grandpa Sal and Uncle Ang came to the United States from Palermo to start their own ice business. It was around 1900, Sal was sixteen and Angelo was seventeen. They had aunts and uncles who lived in Chicago and they needed the Chicago winter for their ice business. Sal's first wife died giving birth to their daughter and seven months later he remarried."

"Are you talking about Nonna Francesca?"

She gasps. "Yes, how did you know?"

"I'm an investigator, mother."

"Then I guess you know it was an arranged marriage, they respected each other but they were never in love."

Daniel writes down everything she says.

"Francesca gave birth to Michael in 1922 and spent the next eighteen years raising Gianna ad Michael as her own. She felt like she had it all, but then Tony...

"I know all about Tony and I know he tried to kill you. Is that true?"

"Yes," she cries. "That's why I didn't want you to know about this. It's terrible."

"I can handle it, but I do have a question."

She sighs.

"Why haven't I met Michael?"

"It was too dangerous."

"What do you mean?"

"I had to keep you safe," she sniffs. "Tony and Anthony are dangerous, they can never know about you."

"Why? I mean, who cares now?"

"Michael inherited everything after Tony killed Sal and his brothers. Tony hated him for it and who's to say Anthony won't seek revenge in his father's name," she says with a heavy sigh. "Daniel, you don't understand."

"What do you mean? Why didn't you tell me this?"

"I don't know, I guess it was just easier to put it all behind me, to pretend it never happened and move on."

"So, what about Anthony Leonetti, what can you tell me about him?"

"He's dangerous, crazy, and if Michael or Francesca find out he is still alive..." her voice cracks. "He's a bad man, Daniel. Please stay away from him."

"Mom, why would he care about me?"

"Because you are my sole heir and when Francesca dies I will inherit half of everything and Tony thinks that half belongs to him."

Daniel's secretary, a new perk since this story broke, walks in and indicates he has a call waiting.

"Mom, I have to go, but I want to talk more about this later, okay?"

"Okay, sweetheart," she says softly and then she ends the call.

Pushing the flashing button on his desk phone he answers, "Donovan."

"Dammit, Daniel, where have you been?" Angus shouts. "I've been trying to call you all night.

Daniel rubs his eyes. "Sorry, man, I've been at work."

Angus sighs.

"I fell asleep, what's going on?"

"Turns out this fishing trip was a cover story for something else."

"Oh?"

"Yeah, the trip to Miami is my bachelor party and Dad is going all out. According to him, the Lara Stuart Modeling Agency has chartered a yacht for a short weekend jaunt to Bermuda and back. We leave tomorrow."

Daniel's jaw drops. "You're kidding."

"No, and there is one more thing. Dad thinks you are a professor friend of mine from the School of Journalism. He can't know you are Daniel Donovan so I had to give him a different name. You are Patrick Beringer."

Daniel sighs. "That makes me nervous. I don't want my parents involved in any of this."

"I had to man. Dad knows all about Daniel Donovan."

Daniel smirks. "Well, at least I have the upper hand," he says and looks around. "Okay, send me the itinerary and I'll see you in Miami Friday afternoon."

"Okay."

"Angus..."

"Yes."

Daniel rubs his face. "Thank you."

"Daniel, there is no love lost between me and my father, you must know that, but be careful. I wouldn't put anything past him."

Eight minutes later Daniel's phone buzzes again and he answers it.

"Donovan."

"The Lara Stuart Modeling Agency is a front for The Consortium. Look up Jerry and Barbara Brown. Find the connection between Lara Stuart and Ian Angus Hall." the call ends.

Daniel writes down everything he heard.

"Daniel!" Bob shouts from his office. "Get in here!"

Daniel walks into his editor's office looking rattled and out of sorts.

"Sit down!" he demands and closes the door behind him. "Would you like to tell me what is going on? I just got a call from Vice Admiral Logan's office wanting to know why you had dinner with Congressman Hall's son last night?"

Daniel sighs and rubs his face. "I was meeting an old friend for dinner."

"This is not just any friend, Daniel, this is Hall's son!" he shouts and then his rant is interrupted by a phone call.

"Hello!" Bob shouts, sighs out loud and looks at Daniel as he hands him his phone. "It's Vice Admiral Logan and he wants to talk to you."

Daniel takes the phone and Bob walks out.

Fifteen minutes later Daniel meets with his team to discuss the situation. "I need someone to investigate the Lara Stuart Modeling Agency and see what you can find about The Consortium. In addition to that, I need someone to investigate the backgrounds of Lara Stuart and Ian Angus Hall to see if there is a connection, and finally...I need someone to find out who Jerry and Barbara Brown are and what, if anything, do they have in common with Lara Stuart."

They all nod their heads and run out.

CHAPTER TEN

February 17, 1989

Carrying his bags from the bedroom to the living room, Daniel notices the red light blinking on his answering machine and even though he normally ignores it, something tells him to check it.

"Hey Daniel, just wanted to let you know my father has some big surprise planned for this weekend. I don't know what it is, but he is really jazzed about it and that makes me nervous. See you when you get down here."

Rubbing his forehead, Daniel exhales. "What am I doing? I must be insane to do this. What if I.A. figures out who I am, what if he figures out I'm Daniel Donovan? I must be completely crazy to do this."

Walking out of his apartment, carrying his bags for the trip to Miami, Daniel is so nervous he can hardly focus. He doesn't know why, but something just feels off about this trip and he has to fight back the urge to call Angus and cancel.

Stepping into the lobby to hail a cab he is surprised to find his team of junior investigators waiting for him.

"Hey guys, what is going on?"

"We have news," Elise says.

"We'll fill you in on the way to the airport," Christian adds.

Daniel looks out the double glass doors, sees a black stretch limousine and smirks. "You shouldn't have."

Christian laughs. "We didn't. My Toyota is behind the stretch."

Daniel's smile turns into a frown.

After loading his bags into Christian's trunk, Daniel climbs into the passenger seat and they drive off.

Christian looks over. "You seem nervous, is everything all right?"

Daniel exhales. "I have a bad feeling about this," he confesses and looks out the window trying to ignore those little hairs on the back of his neck that are tingling. "So, what's up?"

Elise clears her throat. "I have a friend who used to work for the Lara Stuart Modeling Agency in New York. I decided to give her a call to see if she ever heard of Jerry or Barbara Brown."

"Did she?"

"Yes," Elise states. "Jerry and Barbara have a daughter named Emma; she was fourteen when they came to New York to meet Lara Stuart two years ago."

"What happened?"

"Emma did some modeling in her local town when she was little, she was part of the pageant circuit and as she grew older she continued to grab attention. The Lara Stuart Modeling Agency came to her town, held open auditions and they loved her."

"That doesn't sound insidious."

"It wasn't. As far as my friend could tell it was all on the up and up. Lara sent her for head shots, had her meet with her people to be evaluated and even sent her on a few low-level jobs. The feedback was incredible, so Lara invited her to New York."

"Okay, so what happened?"

"Lara offered her a contract, took Emma and her parents to a Broadway show, a basketball game and out to dinner to meet some of her larger clients. Everyone was super impressed, but then they went to a fashion show the day before they were supposed to leave and something strange happened...Emma disappeared."

"What?!"

Elise throws up her hands. "No one knows what happened, I swear! One minute Emma was with Lara to meet the designers and the next thing everyone knew she vanished."

Daniel sighs. "She didn't vanish, she was taken."

They all turn to look at him.

"The police were brought in, the FBI a day later, but Emma was gone without a trace."

Daniel's spidey senses are tingling again. "You said your friend no longer worked there, why did she leave?"

"She said something didn't feel right. She came across some information that suggested Lara Stuart wasn't just in the modeling business..."

"What do you mean?"

"My friend says Lara was running a high-end prostitution and escort service."

Daniel slowly turns his head to look at Elise. "Does she have any proof?"

"Only what happened to her."

"What happened to your friend?"

"Lara offered her a better job, said it could make her a lot of money. My friend decided to do investigating, talked to the other models and they told her not to do it, told her to stay away, and that's when she learned about The Consortium."

Daniel whips his head around to look at her. "The Consortium?"

She nods. "She said one of Lara's models showed up at her house a few days later, said she wanted to talk to her about this job offer Lara made and then she told her what happened to her."

Daniel turns around to face Elise.

"The girl told my friend she came to New York to be a model, auditioned for Lara, and told Lara she would do anything to make it big. Lara arranged for her to do some modeling, got her hooked and then she told her that with some proper training she could be banking $10,000 per month...minimum."

Daniel shakes his head. "A model doesn't start off making that kind of money."

"No, they don't. The girl told my friend she had reservations, said she didn't know if she could trust Lara, but she really needed the money so she agreed to meet with Lara. Lara seemed thrilled, said she would start training right away and then she drove her to the airport. She said she had no idea where she was going, but she had no family, no income, and she was basically living on the streets so anything was better than that."

"The perfect candidate."

"The girl said it took a plane and a helicopter to get there and the place reminded her of a retreat center out in the middle of nowhere, but it was nothing like that and the next thing she knew she was blindfolded, naked, her ankles and wrists were tied to bed posts and she was face down on a large mattress. She remembers hearing a male voice and then she remembers what he did to her."

"Jesus."

"The girl said she felt as if she was having an out of body experience, nothing seemed real, and even though she tried to fight back, tried to protect herself she felt helpless."

"Was she drugged?"

"Possibly, she didn't really know. The only thing she remembers is reaching a point when she felt like it didn't matter anymore."

"So, they broke her."

"I guess."

Daniel exhales. "Jesus."

"The girl said a woman with red hair and dull blue eyes appeared one day and asked her if she had enough, the girl said yes and the second stage of training started. She said it was very different, it was all about learning how to be a lady, how to be subservient and how to please someone in every way. She said it was unsettling, but it was better than before and if this is what it took to get off that island she was willing to do whatever it took."

"But she stayed..."

"The girl said she no longer felt like a human being, she was a commodity, she had a product up for sale and people would bid on her. It was degrading and demeaning at first, but she was in too deep and she couldn't get out. After a little while things changed and she started making more than $10,000 per week. She established her own clientele, five clients, and she figures it's better than living on the streets."

"And the Browns?"

"They are still looking for Emma."

"Do you have a picture?"

Elise hands Daniel a picture. "It's been a year."

Christian parks his car and gets out. "We are going to walk you inside because there is more." Christian says and they each take one of Daniel's bags.

A guy named Adam clears his throat. "So, I have family in Scotland who works for the police and I contacted them to help me investigate Lara Stuart and I.A. Hall."

Daniel slaps him on the back. "Awesome. What did you find out?"

"Well, it's interesting. There is absolutely nothing on Ian Angus Hall, no records whatsoever, but Lara...now she's a different story. Lara Stuart was born Lara Connery in 1932, she was a twin. Her brother's name was Liam. They were Helen and Hugh Connery's fourteenth and fifteenth child, the only girl."

"Yikes!"

"They lived in Glasgow, but moved around a lot. Hugh worked for the ship building industry and split his time between Belfast, Glasgow and Edinburgh before and after the war."

"Which one?"

"Both..."

Daniel eyes widen. "So, he was a military man?"

"An engineer," Adam says. "Hugh had a degree in mechanical engineering from a university in Scotland, but it was more than that. He had a taste for killing and when he led a brigade into battle against the Germans he was so ruthless he changed the outcome of the war, he was given a medal of honor for his heroism and sent home to nurse his injuries. It seems he was exposed to nerve gas."

"Oh."

"Yeah, there's more. There were a rash of murders in Belfast and Glasgow in the late 20's, prostitutes beaten, slaughtered and hung by their ankles from bridges. Hugh was a suspect. When he joined World War II, the killings stopped, but then, without explanation, he was sent home and discharged."

"Sounds suspicious."

"Yeah, I thought so, too, and here is the interesting part. The killings started up again when he returned."

"Did they ever catch him?"

"Nope, but they did find his body in Stirling a few years later."

"His body? I don't understand."

"I guess the apple doesn't fall far from the tree. Liam and Lara, the twins, were real handfuls. Always getting into trouble, always wreaking havoc and things got so bad at one point they were sent off to a reformatory school. Lara got worse, Liam straightened out. A local woodworker took him under his wing, taught him how to use the tools and Liam found his passion. He was really good, so good in fact, he came up with a new oak barrel system for storing scotch that revolutionized the way distilleries stored the amber gold."

"Huh," Daniel says and walks up to security.

Adam continues. "The local woodworker took Liam's barrel to a friend of his, they loved it, and suddenly Liam had a thriving barrel making business. He quit grammar school in eighth grade and rented out a space in the back of a barn to continue making barrels. A year later his friend Alistair Stuart joined him with his older brother and they turned it into a very profitable business."

"Where was his mother and father?"

"Hugh was a mess and Helen left with the children, returned to Dublin, and went to work for her father."

"What did her father do?"

"He was a doctor..." Adam mumbles and checks his notes. "Dr. Edward Donovan."

"Hold on did you say he was from Dublin?"

Adam nods.

Daniel immediately flashes back to high school when he discovered his real father wasn't Ben Beringer, but Patrick Shane Donovan and Patrick's parents were from Dublin.

Adam continues. "Anyway, four years later, in May of 1950 there were two murders. One was Admiral William Kensington in Ayr and the other was Hugh Connery. No one knows what happened, but the reports indicate Kensington returned home unexpectedly, walked in on a man raping his daughter, intervened, and the man stabbed him before cutting her throat. They believe the man was Hugh."

"Christ," Daniel murmurs and takes his bags. "This Alistair Stuart, any connection to Lara?"

"Her husband," Adam says with a smirk.

Daniel stops walking.

Adam puts up his hands. "I already put a call into him."

Daniel's eyes widen. "Jesus, that's big. Good job."

"I know."

Christian clears his throat. "Alright, here's the rest...we couldn't find anything on The Consortium or Damian Santos Delabro, but we are still looking."

"Keep working on it and..." Daniel turns to face his team. "...thanks. You guys are doing a great job. I'll see you when I get back," he says, goes through security, and runs down the main corridor to catch his flight.

CHAPTER ELEVEN

Armed with all this new information, Daniel is restless throughout the flight and is on his fourth beer when the flight attendant tells him it's time to buckle up for the landing and as she takes his empty bottle she slides her name and phone number into his hand.

Stepping off the plane he wonders what happened to Liam and makes a mental note to ask his team to keep looking into that when a cab drives up in front of him.

Climbing inside, he is more than nervous, he is terrified. *If Hall finds out I was the guy Angus had the affair with, or if he finds out I'm Daniel Donovan investigative reporter for The Sun this could be bad, really bad.*

"Where to?" the driver asks.

Daniel looks up and his jaw drops. "Vice Admiral Logan?"

Paul Logan smirks and starts to drive away. "Listen Daniel, I want you to know you are not alone," he says and pulls over to pick up another passenger, but this is not just any passenger, this is one of the guards that stood next to him at the Pentagon, the guard who would lay down his life for the admiral.

Logan drives forward.

"What is going on?"

"We have intelligence that suggests there are escorts and prostitutes on board who will be participating in a special auction. We've had this network under surveillance for years, we're close to nabbing them, but we don't know who is in charge. Daniel, we need you to find out, gather intelligence and help us shut this network down."

"Oh god," Daniel mumbles.

Vice Admiral Logan looks in his rearview mirror. "Daniel, I think this is the same network working the Caribbean and if I'm right they may be the same network who took Arianna Chadwick and Marielle Petrowski. We need to shut them down."

"Jesus."

The large guard scoots over. "Okay, so we are wiring you up," Commander O'Malley says and starts pulling out items from a silver briefcase. "Open your shirt," he says and shows Daniel how to put it on and then he quickly removes it. "There will be security when you arrive, the will search your bags and pat you down, so you will need to do this on your own once on board," he says and opens the bottom of a can of shaving cream to store the wires. "This ring has a panic button," he says and hands Daniel a pinkie ring. "If you feel like your life is in danger, push the signet and we will be there in minutes."

Daniel's eyes widen. "How?"

"We will be following you, we have planted GPS inside your luggage and we have people on the inside."

Vice Admiral Logan pulls over and the large guard gets out. "My engine is about to overheat. I've called for another cab," he says and turns to face Daniel. "Keep calm, we are not going to abandon you."

Daniel nods his head and just like that the engine starts to overheat, Vice Admiral Logan jumps out and starts to act like a crazy man when another cab shows up.

Climbing into the backseat, his new cab takes off.

Arriving at the docks in Miami, Daniel is a nervous wreck, but when he sees Angus standing there waiting for him he seems to calm down. Daniel still has feelings for Angus, feelings he has tried to ignore, but can't. Their relationship in college did matter, but he didn't understand it and he doubts he ever will.

"Patrick!" Angus shouts and waves.

Daniel smirks, holds up his right hand and after going through security he meets up with Angus, hugs him and they climb the ramp to board the massive yacht that looks more like a small cruise ship.

"Good flight?"

Daniel nods. "Great flight."

"So, there has been a bit of a change in our plans."

"Oh?"

"Yeah, I hope you brought your tuxedo; there is a special cocktail party tonight. My father says Lara is hosting a fashion show on the cruise and we have been invited. It's some sort of private show."

Daniel smirks. "I bet."

Angus gives him a sideways look. "We only have an hour to shower and change."

Daniel holds up his garment bag. "No worries."

Angus laughs. "Good."

Angus is quite a handsome guy. With dark black hair, a friendly face, and even friendlier disposition people love him, or at least most people love him. If Daniel had to compare him to anyone he would have to compare him to Kevin Spacey; they could be twins.

"So, this thing tonight is sort of a private gathering for Lara Stuart's most privileged clients. My father paid $20,000 so we could attend."

Daniel's jaw drops.

Angus walks to the door and opens it. "I'm not sure what is going on so be ready for anything, all right?" he says and sighs. "Cocktails are at six and dinner at seven," he says and starts to leave.

"Hold on...why did your father pay $20,000 for cocktails and dinner?"

Angus shakes his head. "I don't know, but whatever happens...don't hold it against me."

Angus leaves and Daniel quickly takes a shower, dries off and puts on the wire Vice Admiral Logan's security gave him. Changing into his tuxedo, he puts on the signet ring and steps out to meet up with Angus looking quite dapper, suave and debonair.

Joining the others in the bar, surrounded by dignitaries, powerful business execs, celebrities and politicians Daniel can't believe his eyes.

"Holy shit," Daniel mumbles and reaches for a glass of champagne. "Angus, these people are some of the most powerful people in the world and I've written stories about them or involving them."

Angus's jaw clenches. "Great."

I.A. joins them with a big smile on his face. "Hello!" he shouts and extends his hand toward Daniel. "I'm..."

Daniel shakes his hand. "Thank you for inviting me Congressman."

Congressman Hall smirks. "It's I.A.," he says and smiles at Angus. "Welcome to Angus' Bachelor Party, glad you could make it on such short notice."

Daniel looks around. "Are all these people here for Angus' party?"

I.A. looks around, nods and laughs. "Yes, they are all good friends of mine and wanted to be here."

"Wow," Daniel mumbles and looks around.

Angus blushes. "Dad, they aren't here for me. They're here for you and you know it."

I.A. slaps Angus on the back. "Maybe," he says and laughs. "When Angus' brother, Sean Michael, bailed on us the other day Angus suggested you. Since it was short notice I sort of fibbed, everyone thinks you are Sean Michael and since they never met him you'll help me keep my little secret, right?"

Daniel smirks. "Sure."

"Okay, good. So, if anyone asks, you are Sean Michael Hall."

Daniel looks at Angus and raises his glass to take another drink. "No problem."

"Wonderful, have a good time," he says and pats Daniel's back.

Daniel looks at Angus. "When are you getting married?"

"Next weekend," Angus says rolling his eyes.

I.A. leans in close. "Angus is marrying a beautiful young lady," he says and slaps Angus on the back again. "I can't wait."

Daniel looks at Angus and taps his glass. "Congrats, man."

I.A. laughs. "I agree," he says and claps his hands together. "On that note...I have some more guests to greet. I'll leave you two to mingle with the girls. If there is someone you are interested in, let me know," he says and winks, but before he leaves he leans in close to Daniel's ear. "Make sure to check out Emme, she's fabulous."

Daniel looks at Emme and cocks his head. There is something familiar about her.

Angus looks and then he shakes his head and looks at I.A. with a sour face. "Dad, what is going on? You said cocktails and dinner, now you are telling us to look around and see if there is someone we are interested in...what's that about?"

"You'll see."

Angus sighs and puts his hands on his hips. "No, Dad, tell me now."

I.A. turns to look at him. "Son, you can have any girl in this room at any time. They are all here for you and they will do anything you want. Spend some time with the girls, talk to them, see what they are good at, and then you can take them back to your room and check them out. They won't tell you 'no'," he smirks. "Tomorrow night you can bid on the girls and take one home for the night," he says and slaps both their shoulders. "Do some research tonight. Patrick should be good at that," he says and then he starts to walk away, stops and turns to look at them. "Once you make your purchase you are stuck with it so take some time to figure it out."

Daniel looks at Angus.

I.A. smiles as he reaches for the hand of another girl. "Have fun."

Daniel's eyes widen.

A beautiful young woman with auburn hair and creamy white skin walks up to Daniel and Angus. "May I offer you a drink?"

They nod their heads.

"Sure, but I have a question first...how large is this yacht?" Daniel asks the young lady.

Angus gives him a strange look.

The girl smirks. "Large. The Glory Be can accommodate up to eighty guests. Where is your cabin?"

"Cabin 201."

The girl smiles. "Mmm, that's nice," she says and glances over at Angus. "And you?"

"Cabin 203."

She smiles and bites her lower lip. "That's even better. You can share and if you decide you have similar tastes..."

"What?" Daniel asks.

Angus clears his throat and then he pulls Daniel off to the side. "Daniel, what are you doing?"

The girl walks over to join them. "There are no rules tonight so if you're interested let me know. We have a strict policy of 'Don't ask, don't tell'."

Angus and Daniel look at each other.

Daniel turns to look at Angus. "Jesus Angus."

Before Angus can reply another woman walks into the lounge. "Gentleman...Ladies, please follow me."

Daniel looks at the four female guests on board and recognizes one is a celebrity, two are politicians and the other...he doesn't know.

"Where is your father? Is he eating with us?" Daniel asks as they follow the crowd into the main dining room and take their seats. Leaning over to Angus, Daniel looks around.

Angus takes a drink of his champagne and then he nods forward. "He's walking toward us right now."

Daniel looks up and sees Congressman Hall shaking everyone's hand as he makes his way through the room and it's obvious that he is well-respected, but even more obvious that he oozes testosterone.

"Son," he says with a slight hint of a Scottish accent, which Daniel never noticed earlier. "Patrick," I.A. adds and then he looks up and smiles. "Senator Holmes." I.A. says and shakes his hand as Congressman Ira Weismann joins them.

"I.A.," he says and shakes it right back. "It's been too long."

"Yes, it has."

Senator Holmes sits down with a loud sigh. "I really need this right now. Thank Lara for me."

Congressman Hall smiles and then he starts talking politics with Weismann and Daniel reaches into his pocket to hit the record button on his hidden recorder and leans back.

I.A. looks at over at them. "Patrick, what did you say your last name was?"

"Beringer," he replies.

I.A. thinks about that for a second. "Why does that name sound so familiar?"

"I don't know."

I.A. waves it off.

Dinner arrives and a fashion show begins. The first course is all about swimsuits. The second course is all about lingerie and the third course is all about leather, stilettos, whips and masks. Walking around the room, the girls distribute leather-bound books.

"What's this?"

Angus shrugs as he flips through it. "It looks like an advertisement for each model. If you read it, it has their picture, tells a story about them and below there is a list of all the things they are known for..." he says, his voice trailing off into a whisper. "Um...wait. This is not a normal list. This is a list of...services."

Daniel looks down. "Oh god," he mumbles searches through the program for the girl, Emme, and when he finds her he places a star next to her name.

I.A. leans over to see what Daniel and Angus are doing, sees that Daniel has put a star next to Emme and smiles. "Oh yes, Emme is fabulous, good choice," he says and nods with a big smile. "But check out the others as well."

Daniel looks at him, and by the time they finish the main course I.A. is so excited he can hardly sit still.

Angus looks at Daniel, swallows hard and exhales. "Jesus, why would my father think this is what I'd want for my Bachelor party?"

Dessert is brought to the tables by the models and now they are wearing masks, their bodies covered in body paint from the waist up, wearing only bikini bottoms and stilettos. The only way to identify them is by the number on the back of their bikini bottoms.

A woman with red hair and blue eyes moves to stand behind the podium. "Good Evening, hopefully you have all had a chance to look over the program and select the items you'd like to try this evening..."

Daniel looks around and spots another girl who looks familiar, looks at her number and then he looks her up.

"What's going on?" Angus asks.

"I don't know, but there is something about that girl, too—

Daniel stops talking and looks over the girl's bio.

"Her name is Adara," Daniel mumbles reading from the book. "That means beauty in Greek and virgin in Arabic," he says and looks up at her once again.

I.A. leans in front of Angus and looks at them. "Tonight is all about having a good time. Get to know the girls. Tomorrow is when the fun really begins."

For the next hour or two everyone mingles, flirts and chats, but then Daniel runs across a girl who looks just like Marielle Petrowski and his heart skips a beat.

"What's your name?"

"Mariam," she says shyly and it's obvious she is not comfortable in this environment like the other girls.

Looking around, Daniel scans the room for Adara, who he believes is Arianna Chadwick, but he's too late. The girls are starting to leave with the guests.

I.A. has two girls, both red heads, and after saying good night he leaves with them.

Walking over to the bar, Daniel orders a scotch and just as the bartender hands him the glass the young Emme joins him.

"I heard you were looking for me."

Daniel almost spits out his drink.

Emme smiles and when she does it suddenly occurs to Daniel that Emme is Emma and he immediately grabs her hand. "Come with me."

"Sure," she giggles.

Leading her to his private suite he opens the door, ushers her inside and then he closes the door and locks it.

"I'm not going anywhere; you don't have to lock the door."

"Habit," he says and walks into the bathroom to splash some cold water on his face.

While he's gone, she removes her mask and when he walks out of the bathroom, sees her, he hands her his robe and orders her to put it on as he walks over to his briefcase to take out the picture of Emma.

When he turns around she is naked, standing in front of him and it's as if she is waiting for instructions.

Daniel holds up his hands. "Hold on," he stutters and wraps the robe around her. "I want to talk first," he says and then he pulls her down to sit next to him.

Emme looks nervous.

Daniel senses it and turns to face her. "Are you all right?"

She drops her head. "I'm sorry. I don't understand what is going on. No one ever wants to talk."

"Oh," he says and laughs. "I guess I'm new at all this, so hopefully you can cut me a little slack."

She smiles.

Daniel waits for a second, then he takes out the picture to show her. "Do you recognize this girl?"

Emme immediately reaches up to cover her mouth. "Where did you get that?"

He looks at her. "Your mother and father, Barbara and Jerry Brown."

Her jaw drops and then she slowly turns to look at him as tears well up in her eyes. "That can't be true. My parents were killed in a car accident."

Daniel's eyes widen. "Who told you that?"

"Lara," she says. "Lara said my parents were killed in a car accident!" she shouts and then she looks at their picture again, starts to cry harder and her hands start shaking.

Daniel immediately drops to his knees in front of her. "Emma, that's not true. Your parents have been looking for you, they've been to the police, hired a private investigator and when they couldn't find you they contacted a man named 'Carl' who contacted me."

"Who are you?"

"My name is Daniel I am an investigative journalist with The Sun."

Emma looks shocked, gets up to start pacing the room and starts to panic. "They can't know about this," she says nodding toward the door. "They can't know any of this."

"Stop," he says sounding authoritative. "Tell me what is going on, I want to help."

She drops her head. "I don't know what to do...if Li—

"Who?"

She sighs and starts ringing her hands together. "If the owner finds out he will punish me and I don't want to go back there."

"Owner? Is the owner on board?" Daniel asks.

"Yes."

"Can you point him out to me or describe him to me?"

She gives him a curious look. "I..." she walks away, starts pacing, and begins to cry again. "He will kill me."

Daniel sees how terrified she is. "I won't let that happen."

She looks up at him. "You promise?"

"I promise."

She thinks about it, bites her lower lip and sighs. "What do you want to know?"

Daniel reaches for his recorder. "Anything you want to tell me."

Emme starts to pace again. "Being a model was my dream, but this is not what I meant," she starts and over the next two hours she tells him how Lara got her the head shots, put her in acting classes and even introduced her to some of the top models, but then she told me that I could make triple the amount of money if I agreed to some special training and when I found out about my parents I figured I had no choice.

"The next thing I knew we were on a plane and then we took a helicopter to a private island, but the training wasn't what I thought," she says her voice dropping. "It wasn't training to be a super-model; it was training for this," she says and starts crying.

Daniel tries to comfort her.

"If I don't get a good review I have to go back to the island."

"What do you mean?"

Emme drops her head. "I get paid based upon my reviews."

"Emme, I will give you a great review no matter what, but I need you to talk to me. What happened to you while on the island?"

Emma looks at him, searches his eyes and the next thing he knows she starts telling him everything that happened from the moment her parents left all the way up to tonight. After another hour or so, he is so shocked he can hardly believe this is real, that this type of thing really happens.

"So, this is a well-organized human trafficking ring," he mumbles and thanks god he remembered to press play on his recorder.

This is what Vice Admiral Logan was looking for, this is what he was looking for and suddenly it all hits him.

"Do you think the others would talk to me, tell me their real names and help me figure this all out?"

"I don't know."

There is a knock at the door and they both jump.

Scrambling to hide everything, he quickly undresses, Emme gets into the bed and he puts on the robe, but when he opens the door he sees Angus with Mariam and quickly ushers them inside.

Seeing Emme, the second girl looks nervous, hesitant even, but after Emme tells her what is going on the girl looks at Daniel and then she bursts into tears.

"Do you know your real name?" Daniel asks cautiously.

The girl nods her head and Emme kneels up to hug her and reassure her everything will be all right.

The girl looks up at Daniel and Angus. "My name is Marielle Petrowski."

"Oh god," Angus mumbles.

She looks up at him. "God doesn't exist."

Daniel looks at her and slowly drops down in the chair next to her. "Yes, he does or I wouldn't be here."

Marielle and Emma hug one another.

Slowly pulling himself together, Daniel turns to face the girls. "Are there others like you? Others who were lied to or abducted, others who would be willing to talk to me or talk to you?" he asks and his hand goes into his hair. "We have to get as much information as possible so we can put an end to all this and get you all home, but I can't do this without you."

"We can try. We are all going to a spa on the island in the morning we could talk to the others while we're there."

Daniel looks at Marielle. "Is Arianna on board?"

Marielle looks shocked. "You know about Arianna?"

Daniel nods his head. "Her father has never stopped looking for her either."

"She's on board, but she isn't doing well."

Emma looks at Daniel. "She's had to go back to the island several times, I don't think she is working out."

Daniel looks at Angus and then he nods and looks back at the girls. "You can't let anyone know what is going on, we have to keep this quiet. I want to help you, I want to stop this from happening to others, but I need you to trust me."

The girls nod their heads.

"Okay, so here is the plan..."

The girls leave and Daniel takes a deep breath, looks at Angus and swallows. "We are taking a big chance here."

"I know, but Daniel if my father finds out I am involved in this he won't hesitate to kill me and make you watch before he kills you."

Daniel starts to get worried about Angus being there and tells him it's okay to bail out, but Angus wants nothing to do with that.

The next morning, Angus takes Daniel's recorder and goes off to the beach with his father while Daniel joins the group to do some shopping and when they get back Emma wastes no time in finding him and plants a big kiss on him.

I.A. laughs and slaps him on the back. "Told you Emme was fabulous."

Handing Daniel his tiny recorder, Angus gives him a look and Daniel knows there must be something really good on there.

Emma tugs on Daniel's hand to lead him away and hands him another recorder. "Once they started talking they didn't stop."

Daniel nods, takes the recorder and adjourns to his cabin where he spends the next three and a half hours listening to the recordings Angus and Emma made.

CHAPTER TWELVE

Early Sunday morning Daniel hears a loud noise that sounds like a helicopter, steps out on his balcony, and watches one land on the top deck. Looking around, he sees Miami off in the distance and then he hears a knock at his door and Angus walks in.

"Okay, here is your camera. You've got all the photos of the girls, the young men and all the guests, what else can I do?"

"Nothing. The rest of this is on me," Daniel mumbles when there is a knock at the door and he quickly shoves all his things in the hidden compartment under his clothes.

I.A. walks in. "So how are you two fine gentlemen this morning?" I.A. asks. "And how was last night?"

Daniel smiles. "I had a great time, thank you for inviting me."

I.A.'s eyes widen and Daniel isn't sure, but he thinks I.A. giggles. "Fantastic! Fantastic!" he shouts and turns to look at Angus. "And you?"

Angus looks at his father, swallows and then he stands up straighter. "I'm trying, dad."

"That's all I ask, son," he says and then he slaps Angus on the back. "Listen, I need to take off. I'll see you next weekend, okay?"

Angus nods his head. "Can't wait."

I.A. leaves and Daniel follows him to the door to make sure he's gone before he turns to face Angus. "What did he mean when he said he needs to take off?"

Angus shrugs. "The helicopter is for him. He's leaving."

With a shake of his head and a slight smirk of disbelief, Daniel walks over to Angus. "If everything goes as planned you won't need to marry that girl, I'll make sure of it," he says and presses the signet on his ring.

Angus sighs. "My father brought me here because he is hoping to cure me of being gay; he thinks if I do things with women I will forget all about being with men."

"Angus."

Angus shakes his head, thrusts his hand into his hair and looks like he is going to cry. "What am I going to do?" he asks and walks over to the slider to look out at the ocean. "My father is never going to stop watching me, he is never going to leave me alone and now I have to marry this woman I have no feelings for *and* give her two children," he mumbles sounding defeated and sits down on the edge of the bed to drop his head between his hands.

Daniel walks over to him. "I'm sorry, Angus."

Angus shakes his head and turns to look at Daniel. "I know you never loved me like I loved you."

"That's not true," Daniel says surprising himself at how true that statement is.

Angus looks at him. "It's not?"

Daniel shakes his head and then he sighs. "No," he mumbles. "I thought you were the best thing that ever happened to me, but there is this other part of me and I can't ignore it."

Angus nods. "Do you think you could ever see us together again?"

Daniel smiles. "I don't know, but I do know one thing...I would hate to lose our friendship."

Angus smiles. "Yeah, me, too."

The yacht pulls into its slip, comes to a stop and within seconds there is a loud raucous going on outside the cabins, loud voices ordering everyone out of their rooms and when Daniel opens his door he is shocked to see armed men in black t-shirts and black combat pants with masks on.

"Get out!" a man orders and forces Daniel and Angus out of their rooms.

"What is going on?" Daniel asks as he is being forced down on his knees and in walks Vice Admiral Paul Logan who ignores both Daniel and Angus, making sure to treat them the same as all the others.

"You are all under arrest!" he shouts.

Within seconds they are handcuffed with zip ties and are being hauled to their feet.

"Move it!"

Everyone is ushered out to large vans and taken to the police station to be interviewed, but when its Daniel's turn he is taken out to a large black SUV and they leave.

"Hold on, where is Angus?"

The Vice Admiral and U.S. Attorney Peyton Logan turn back to look at him.

"He's with the others."

Four hours later, Daniel leaves the police station in an unmarked silver sedan.

"What happened to Angus?"

Peyton Logan turns to look at him. "I.A. had him out in less than fifteen minutes. His brother, Sean Michael handled his release."

"Did you get what you needed?"

Peyton laughs. "Almost...we thought we'd get Hall, Weismann, Holmes and a few more but they weren't on board."

Daniel looks at him. "They weren't?"

Peyton looks at him. "Were they?"

Daniel thinks about this for a second, thinks about Angus and in that tiny little moment makes a decision that will change their lives forever.

Boarding a private jet, Daniel spends the entire flight telling them everything he knows and when they land he goes back to his office, develops the film, makes copies of the recordings and then he hands everything over to the Logan's.

The story breaks the next day and it makes international news.

Bob and Elise walk in with a bottle of champagne only to find Daniel staring out the window.

"Congratulations!" they shout.

Daniel drops his head. "Yeah, thanks."

Elise tilts her head. "Hey, what's wrong?" she asks and walks over to stand next to Daniel. "Daniel, you should be on cloud nine. Your story has made international news, you broke up one of the largest human trafficking networks the world has ever seen and you single-handedly reunited all those young people with their families. Arthur Chadwick can't stop talking about you. He has his child back; they all have their children back."

Daniel nods his head.

Bob narrows his eyes. "Daniel, Logan and his team have everyone in custody. Charges are expected by this afternoon. You just broke the story of a lifetime. You did it! You finally nabbed the big one!"

Daniel tries for a smile and turns to walk around his desk. "Don't get me wrong. I'm glad the victims are safe," he says and starts to clean up his desk. "Did they arrest Lara Stuart yet?"

"I don't know," Bob replies watching Daniel suspiciously. "We should know something any minute...hey, are you alright?"

Daniel sighs as he recalls how I.A. left the yacht by helicopter with Victor VonMeister, Phillip Barnes, Robert Holmes and Ira

Weismann. "So, what do you think is going to happen? Do you think Lara will tell the feds what they need to know?"

Elise shakes her head.

Bob walks over to Daniel and pats him on the back. "Listen Daniel, I think you need to get out of town for a little while. The fate of Lara Stuart and everyone on board that yacht is now in the hands of the U.S. Attorney," he mumbles. "Why don't you go home and visit your mom or take a vacation."

Daniel looks at Bob for a second and then he nods his head. "Peyton Logan suggested the same thing. I think he wants me out of town, too."

Bob looks at him. "Listen to us."

Daniel nods. "He suggested I take a sabbatical, even offered to help me find something for a couple of months."

"Jesus, this must be bigger than I thought." Bob mumbles. "What are you going to do?" he asks.

Daniel sighs. "I don't know. Maybe I'll go back to my alma mater. They extended an invitation to become an adjunct professor in the School of Journalism, maybe I should take them up on it."

Bob nods his head. "Sounds like it might be the perfect distraction…" he mumbles and starts to leave. "Let me know what you decide…" he says and then he stops and remembers something. "Oh yeah, I almost forgot. Arthur Chadwick sent this for you," he says and hands Daniel an envelope.

Daniel opens it, pulls out several papers and reads the letter. "A personal note of thanks and…" he holds up a check. "Jesus."

Bob smiles. "You deserve it."

Daniel looks at the check with six zeros and sighs.

Bob pats him on the shoulder.

Daniel drops his head and thinks about Angus. "Do you think Lara Stuart will cooperate?"

"No."

Daniel's eyes widen and he thinks about that, thinks about what that means for Angus, for him and in a nanosecond, he knows what he has to do.

Grabbing his coat, his briefcase and his keys, Daniel walks up to Bob and pats him on the back. "I'll let you know my decision, you let me know when charges are filed."

Seeing Daniel walk toward the elevator, Christian runs after him holding a handful of pictures. "Daniel!" he shouts. "Hey, don't leave yet. Alistair Stuart finally got back to me. He sent this…" he says and holds up a large envelope as he jumps into the elevator with Daniel. "The pictures are old and the images are grainy, but this is all he could find. Inside this envelope are pictures of Lara Connery and Liam Connery. There is also a picture of their youngest brother, Will."

Daniel opens it, pulls out the pictures and his eyes almost pop out of his head. "Jesus, that's Lara Stuart and..."

"Alistair thinks Liam killed his father, he thinks he killed Admiral Kensington, too. He thinks Kensington was an accident, but Hugh was not. Alistair believes Hugh was killing those girls, he believes Liam caught him in the act and killed him. He said Liam disappeared right before Kensington and Mr. Connery were found. He said he came to the shop where they built their barrels, took money out of the safe and left. That was the last time Alistair saw Liam. It was as if he disappeared off the face of the earth."

Daniel looks at the picture of Lara and Liam Connery again.

"Alistair told me one more thing...Moira Montgomery, Lord Charles Montgomery's daughter, disappeared the same night Liam did. Alistair thinks they ran off together and no one knows this, but she was pregnant at the time."

Daniel looks at him. "How pregnant?"

"Three months..."

"So, that means, if the child survived he or she would have been born in December of 1948."

The elevator doors open.

Daniel looks at him. "Thanks man, I needed this."

Christian nods. "If Alistair Stuart is right this guy Liam has gone to great lengths to hide his past. You need to be careful."

Chapter Thirteen

Daniel leaves for the airport, Vice Admiral Logan's men watching him, but instead of getting on the plane Daniel changes his plans. Avoiding the watchful eye of Logan's men, he hands his ticket to Christian, they have a little chat and Daniel disappears into the restroom while Christian boards the plane.

Waiting for Logan's men to leave, Daniel jumps into a waiting car and Bob drives him straight to the same hotel where Sabrina Alphonso confronted Hall more than fourteen years ago.

"Thanks Bob."

Bob looks at Daniel. "I know how you feel about this," he mumbles. "Hell Daniel, I feel the same way, but are you sure this is the right way to handle this?"

Daniel nods his head. "I have no choice. I have to protect Angus," he says and walks into the lobby of the hotel, nods to the hotel manager and takes a seat until all his guests arrive.

A half hour later Robert Holmes arrives with Ira Weismann chatting about who summoned them and why. Watching them from across the salon, Daniel can't help but smirk, but there is someone else who still needs to arrive and when he sees him walk through the double doors of the hotel he takes a deep breath and prepares for the biggest moment of his life.

"Gentleman," the hotel manager says greeting the three men. "Will you follow me?"

Weismann, Holmes, and Hall follow exchanging glances and wondering what in the hell is going on as the manager leads them to the private dining room.

"Did you summon us here?" Weismann asks Hall.

"No," he sneers.

"Well, who did?"

Daniel steps into the room. "I did."

Seeing Daniel, Hall stops talking, narrows his eyes and then he puts his hands on his hips. "What in the hell are you doing here?"

"Have a seat," Daniel orders.

Hall's eyes almost pop out of his head. "Excuse me?"

Daniel walks by him. "You heard me, take a seat," he says and stands in front of him daring him to say something back when six large men walk in wearing black fatigues.

Fully armed and ready to do whatever they are told to do, the guards walk up to I.A. and seeing them I.A. has a sudden change of heart, holds up his hands and takes a seat at the round table in the middle of the room.

"What is going on here, Patrick?"

Ira Weismann looks at Daniel. "Patrick, did you call us here today?"

Daniel looks Ira and then he turns to look at I.A. and smirks. "First, my name is not Patrick Beringer, it's Daniel Donovan. Second, I am an investigative journalist with The Sun."

I.A. immediately stands, Ira leans forward looking sick to his stomach and Robert Holmes looks shocked.

"I knew something wasn't right with you!" I.A. shouts. "I knew it!" he shouts again.

"Oh, shut up, I.A., you never suspected Patrick, or rather Daniel, was an investigator...you thought he was gay!"

"You shut up, Ira," I.A. spews right back.

Daniel holds up his hands. "Enough!" he shouts and looks at Ira and I.A., points and orders the men to sit down.

I.A. ignores him, Ira immediately complies.

Daniel looks at I.A. and clears his throat. "I said SIT DOWN!"

I.A. looks at him and moves to stand on the opposite side of the table from Daniel. "Just who do you think you are? You don't tell me what to do, you don't order me around and you sure as hell don't get to tell me to sit down. No one orders me to do anything, do you understand?"

There is an uncomfortable silence in the room as Ira and Robert watch Daniel narrow his eyes, rest his hands down on the table and leans forward.

"You can either sit down on your own or I will order my men to make you sit...you choose."

I.A. looks at Daniel, sees the look in his eyes and considers his options, but when he sees Daniel turn toward the six guards he decides to sit.

Annoyed and angry, I.A. waves his hand in front of him. "This is ridiculous. Who do you think you are? What is going on here? What do you want?"

Daniel nods to someone lurking in the dark corner, a door opens, and five people walk in carrying file boxes, sets them down in front of Daniel and leave.

One is marked I.A. Hall, two is marked Robert Holmes, three is marked Ira Weismann, four is marked Lara Stuart, and the last one is marked Damian Santos Delabro.

I.A. points and wags his finger from side to side. "What's this?"

"These boxes are filled with evidence, evidence I've collected on each of you, evidence I will hand over to the U.S. Attorney and Vice Admiral Logan as well as my editor, Bob, at The Sun if you don't comply with my wishes.

Robert Holmes swallows, Ira Weismann leans back and rubs his chin and I.A. leans back to look at Daniel.

"Evidence? What evidence?"

Daniel opens the box marked "Robert Holmes" and takes out a piece of paper. "How about evidence tying Robert Holmes to the brutal rape of Sabrina Alphonso, Christina Harris, and Adele Stevenson," he says and sets the paper inside to pull out a thick file. "Depositions, pictures, and DNA samples," he says and holds up the items. "...linking Holmes to those raps as well as sixteen more."

Robert Holmes squirms in his chair.

"I don't believe you!" I.A. shouts.

Daniel nods his head. "Okay, then how about this..." he says and takes out another thick file. "What would Vice Admiral Logan say when he finds out the Chairman of the ethics committee received wire transfers from Dr. David Stone and The Stone Infertility Institute in the amount of—

"Alright!" Robert Holmes shouts and shakes his head. "I believe you. What do you want?"

Ira swallows hard and looks at Holmes. "Did you take a bribe from Stone? Why?"

Holmes looks at Daniel and then he looks at Ira. "Stone wanted to get Maternix fast-tracked through the FDA approval process. I..." he shrugs. "I helped it along."

Ira exhales and looks at Daniel who is opening a box with his name on it. "Stop!" Ira shouts. "I don't need proof, I believe you."

Daniel smirks, turns toward I.A. and narrows his eyes. "What about you?"

I.A. gets up, walks over to Daniel and opens the box with his name on it, sees it is filled with files and runs his fingers over the tabs marked Hugh and Helen Connery, Lara Connery Stuart,

Leonetti Trucking and Transport, Angus, Chicago, and Beatrice Ayers, closes the box and exhales. "What do you want?"

"Take your seat and I'll tell you."

With his hand in his hair, I.A. turns on his heel and walks back, sits down, and rests his elbows on the table.

"By now you know that Lara Stuart and most of the guests on board the Glory Be have been arrested and charged with more than twenty-one Federal charges from child exploitation, human trafficking, prostitution and obscenity. In addition, the young women and men who were victimized by Stuart have been deposed and reunited with their families."

I.A. pushes his chair back and stands, but the moment he does the six men surround him and now he is beyond angry. "This is ridiculous! If you are going to arrest us, then do it already. Why are you toying with us?"

Daniel looks at him and shakes his head. "No, I've decided to keep your names out of it, but how long will depend on you."

All three men look at him.

"There is no statute of limitation for what you've done and even though Vice Admiral Logan and U.S. Attorney Peyton Logan would love to take you down I'm not going to be the one to help them...not yet."

Senator Holmes looks at Daniel. "What do you want?"

Daniel looks at him. "I have a proposition for you and if you choose to accept it I will keep your names out of it, but if you refuse my men will take you to the proper authorities and I will hand over all my evidence. Evidence that will destroy you, your families, and your careers."

I.A. thinks about it for a few seconds, thinks about the tabs inside the box and slams his hand down on the table. "Fine! What do you want?"

Daniel tosses out three envelopes. "Open them!" he shouts and two men walk in to join them. "There are multiple versions of this story and I haven't decided which will be released to the public. I am leaving that up to you."

"Leave me out of it. I'll do whatever you want," Robert Holmes cries.

Daniel looks at him and nods.

"Me, too," Ira relents.

I.A. looks at them and then he looks at Daniel. "How do we know we can trust you? What assurances do we have that you will not expose us even after we agree to give you what you want?"

Daniel sits down, reaches for his scotch and takes a drink. "You don't," he says as a matter of fact. "You'll have to trust me."

I.A. rubs his chin, looks at Robert Holmes and Ira Weismann, and exhales. "Fine, tell us what you want."

"Each of you will be required to wire $12,000 per month to an account in Switzerland and I want you," he says turning to face I.A. Hall, "to leave Angus alone, have nothing more to do with him."

"He's my son, why would I do that?"

"That's part of the deal take it or leave it."

Robert Holmes clears his throat. "Fine, anything else?"

"If you go against my wishes, if anything happens to Angus, to me, my family, or my editor I will release all the evidence to Vice Admiral Paul Logan, U.S. Attorney Peyton Logan and two others as well as post it all in The Sun."

Robert Holmes and Ira Weismann immediately stand and are escorted out, but I.A. isn't so easily swayed.

Daniel stands. "When I leave this room, your time will be up," he says and starts toward the double doors when I.A. slams his hand down on the table and stands to confront Daniel.

"You might think you've won, but I'm a powerful man and I will find out where you've hidden all the evidence," he says, walks over to Daniel and pokes him in the chest. "When I do, I'm coming after you and I will make you pay for what you've done."

Daniel looks away and exhales.

I.A.'s eyes immediately flash with anger. "And one more thing...you'd better hope nothing gets leaked because if it does U.S. Attorney Peyton Logan, Vice Admiral Paul Logan, nor your mother will be able to find all your body parts."

Daniel smirks and then he shakes his head. "Is that what Tony Leonetti taught you?"

I.A.'s eyes widen.

"Or is that what your father taught you?" Daniel asks and leans up against I.A.'s ear.

I.A. freezes and then he steps back and refuses to look Daniel in the eye. "I don't know what you are talking about."

Daniel notices his reaction immediately. "Like I said when I leave...your time is up."

I.A. glares at him.

"I.A., you can threaten me all you want, but it doesn't matter. I hold your freedom in my hands and if you make one move against me, my family, my friends or Angus I will not hesitate to use it and believe me, Li—

I.A.'s eyes flash up to meet Daniel's.

Daniel clears his throat. "Believe me, I.A., I know more than was in those files."

Daniel starts to walk away and I.A. clears his throat.

"Did my son know what you were up to?"

"No," Daniel says, turns to face him and shakes his head. "I would never do that to Angus."

I.A. narrows his eyes. "You are the one, aren't you? The one he had the affair with?"

Daniel looks at him. "Yes."

I.A. nods his head. "I knew it."

"Leave Angus alone," Daniel says, turns and leaves as I.A. walks out the other door with the man lurking in the corner.

CHAPTER FOURTEEN

June 4, 1989

"I don't want you to go," Tierney McCort whispers into Jackie Logan's ear. "I want you to stay with me, come to Dublin with me, marry me. I want to spend the rest of my life with you."

Jackie laughs, scoots out of Tierney's bed and walks into the bathroom.

"Tierney," she replies pulling her long curly caramel colored blond hair into a ponytail. "What would I do in Dublin?"

Tierney roll over on his side to look at her. "I don't know, you could get a job as a nurse, stay at home, go back to school...I don't care as long as we're together."

She turns on the water to take a shower and he quickly jumps out of bed to join her.

"Why are you being so stubborn and bull headed about this?"

Jackie looks at him. "Because I can't concentrate around you, you know that; especially when you're..." her eyes slowly scan his body. "...naked," she says, smiles, and slides her hands up his naked chest to wrap her arms around his neck. "You know what you do to me," she mumbles.

He smiles and slides his hands around her naked body. "I want to do more things to you," he whispers and starts to kiss her.

She drops her head back and giggles. "I'm going to be late for work."

"I have connections, it will be fine," he whispers and that's all she needs to hear.

A half hour later, Jackie is scrambling to get dressed and out the door when Tierney walks out of the bathroom wearing only a towel.

With a loud sigh, she sits down on the edge of the bed to put on her shoes. "Tierney, we talked about this. You go to Dublin to oversee the building of the hospital you helped design and while you're away I'll finish up my Master's degree. We talked about this it's the best solution and when you get back we can start our life together," she says, grabs her purse and moves to stand in the doorway. "It's the perfect plan."

Turning to walk out of his bedroom, Jackie walks into the kitchen to fill her to travel mug with coffee when Tierney joins her wearing a pair of button fly jeans with the top button left open on purpose.

"Is this because of Brigitte or your mother?"

Jackie spills the coffee and exhales. "No," she mumbles.

He looks at her and knows she isn't telling him the truth. "What did Brigitte say to you last night?"

She glances up at him and he blocks the doorway making it impossible for her to leave. "Ugh," she exhales. "Fine."

He folds his arms across his chest and waits.

Looking down at the countertop, Jackie runs her finger down the seam of the tile and exhales. "Brigitte told me I didn't belong in your world," she confesses, her voice cracking. "She said you deserved to be with someone who understood your needs and I would never be able to do that...maybe she's right," Jackie says with a slight shrug and kisses his cheek knocks him off guard and she sneaks past him.

Stunned, he turns to follow. "You know that's not true," he says and looks at Jackie with a concerned look on his face.

Tierney McCort is the most beautiful man Jackie has ever known. Tall, with dark brown wavy hair, a gorgeous smile and the most beautiful brown eyes she has ever seen. The attraction was instant, the love that has grown between them is powerful, and the truth is...he is the man of her dreams.

"Do I?" she asks reaching for her coat. "I don't know Tierney, maybe Brigitte is right...maybe I'm not the right girl for you."

"Jackie, stop."

She stops and looks at him. "Listen, Brigitte is your sister-n-law and she hasn't liked me from day one. She thinks I'm having an affair with your brother for god's sake, my boss!" she shouts and shakes her head. "I know Andrew is her husband and your brother, but I would never do that I hope you believe me."

"I know," he says and reaches for her to hug her. "Brigitte's insecurities are really putting a damper on things."

"Why can't she leave us alone?"

"I don't know," Tierney mumbles and leans back to look at Jackie. "Andrew says she is a control freak. He thinks this behavior has something to do with her father," he says and shakes his head. "They had a big fight after we left last night."

"Oh no."

Tierney exhales. "Tegan and I think it's about time. Andrew needs to get a backbone where Brigitte is concerned. He needs to put her in her place. Brigitte causes problems for all of us."

Jackie sighs. "Great, if they fought about me it will only add fuel to the fire where Brigitte is concerned. Now she's never going to let this go."

Tierney wraps his arms around Jackie. "I don't care what Brigitte thinks."

Jackie kisses him. "Yes, but I do," she mumbles and opens the front door. "I need to get going. Today is my last day at the hospital and they are throwing me a party."

Tierney sighs, follows her and then he kisses her one more time. "Fine, I'll see you after work."

"Okay," Jackie mumbles and does her best to give him a smile as she walks down the front steps. "Love you," she sings waving to him and then she realizes what she just said and blushes bright red. "I mean..."

Tierney smiles. "I love you, too," he sings and waves to Jackie as she pulls away.

Driving to the hospital Jackie can't stop thinking about Tierney and sighs. "Maybe Brigitte's right. Maybe I don't belong in Tierney's world."

Arriving at the hospital, Jackie is surprised by the large party in her honor. She had no idea so many people would be there, no idea her sister Carrie and Tierney's sister Tegan would be there, and no idea there would be so much food.

"Wow Jackie, I think St. Matthew's loves you," Carrie says giving her sister a hug.

"What are you doing here?"

Carrie smiles. "Tegan called, said today was your last day and invited me to the party. Since you don't tell us anything, I have to go behind you back to find out what you're up to."

Jackie smirks.

Tegan walks up to Jackie and hugs her to her side. "We thought we'd join the party here, take you out shopping and meet up with Tierney for dinner."

"Oh really?"

Tegan giggles. "Uh huh!"

Carrie notices a little hesitation in Jackie and narrows her eyes, but waits until Tegan leaves to inquire.

"Hey, what's wrong?"

Jackie leads her away from the others. "Tierney brought up Dublin again."

Carrie sighs. "Oh..." she mumbles and turns to look at Jackie. "Have you told Blake about Tierney yet?"

Jackie shakes her head.

Carrie's jaw drops. "Jackie! Why haven't you told him?"

Jackie shrugs and walks out on the terrace.

Carrie follows.

"I wanted to tell Blake a million times, but it's always on the phone and I think this is a conversation we should have face-to-face."

Carrie reaches for her arm. "Jackie, you need to tell him. This isn't right," she mumbles. "Unless..."

"Unless what?"

Carrie sighs. "Unless you are second thoughts about Tierney."

Jackie looks away. "Carrie, what if I'm not the right girl for him? What if Brigitte is right?"

"Oh, Jesus, Jackie. Why are you going to let Brigitte McCort get in your head? She's a controlling little bitch who can't mind her own business, you know that."

Jackie sighs. "I know you're right, but she won't stop. It's like every time I turn around she is doing something, saying something or causing some sort of problem. It's too much."

"Jacqueline Elizabeth Logan, what is wrong with you?"

Jackie laughs and then she shakes her head. "Carrie, Tierney comes from a prominent, powerful, wealthy family, why would he want someone like me? Brigitte has a point."

"Did I just hear you tell your sister you think Brigitte is right?" Tegan interjects walking out on the terrace to join them. "Oh, Jackie, if you believe that then maybe you aren't the right one for Tierney."

Carrie and Jackie turn to look at her.

Tegan takes a deep breath and exhales. "My family is not like Brigitte's family. Our father made sure we were grounded, he made sure we understood the meaning of hard work and he never gave us anything unless we needed it. Brigitte is not like us, she grew up surrounded by wealth, surrounded by privilege and her father..." she sighs. "Don't even get me started about him."

Carrie narrows her eyes. "Congressman Hall? What is wrong with the Congressman?"

Tegan rolls her eyes. "Let's just put it this way...Brigitte is just like him. Hateful, evil, and controlling."

Jackie narrows her eyes.

"If you want to know why Brigitte is such a control freak look at her past."

"What do you mean?" Jackie asks.

"From what Andrew told us I.A. was never around when Brigitte was growing up. I.A. was from the old boys' network, he was popular, and he never believed rules applied to him. He had constant affairs, humiliated Beatrice and their family on more than one occasion. Kennedy's womanizing was nothing compared to I.A.'s. Brigitte blamed Beatrice for everything at first, but then I.A. rejected Brigitte, humiliated her, and chose an eighteen-year-old red headed college girl over her. Brigitte was never the same after that and when she found out about all the other girls she blamed them for breaking up their family. You are a young college girl, you have impressed Andrew, he talks about you all the time, and now you are dating Andrew's brother. Brigitte doesn't want you anywhere near her family. She thinks you are going to do to her what those other college girls did to her family."

Carrie exhales.

Jackie bites her lip. "I'm not interested in Andrew like that. I have great respect for him and I've learned a lot from him, but I—

"I know, but this doesn't have anything to do with you it's all about her." Tegan interjects with a loud sigh. "Andrew would never be unfaithful to Brigitte, he is completely in love with her, but she won't let it go. It's as if you have triggered something inside her, something no one understands."

Jackie exhales. "Brigitte told me I didn't belong in Tierney's world. She wants me to leave him alone."

Tegan exhales. "Listen, Jackie...Brigitte doesn't have a say in Tierney's life."

"I don't want to cause problems in your family."

"You won't. There is nothing to worry about. Not anymore."

"What does that mean?"

She looks at Jackie. "Did Tierney ever tell you the history of our family?"

Jackie shakes her head. "No, why?"

She smirks. "Then it's about time you know. Our great grandfather, Ryan McCort, came to Lake Forest in 1905 with his twin brother Gavin. They came to work for their uncles, the Kelly brothers, who owned all this land. Asher Kelly was a lawyer, Padrig was a surgeon, and Jedidiah owned the county's first newspaper. Gavin and Ryan spent ten years working for Jedidiah, but they wanted more and with Jedidiah's help they started McCort Hall Printing and Publishing."

"Any connection to McCort-Hall Printing and Publishing?"

"The same."

Jackie's draw drops. "Your family owns a publishing company?"

"They did, but Ryan sold it all to Gavin in 1920 to start McCort Construction."

"Wow."

Tegan smiles. "Gavin McCort is Brigitte's great grandfather."

Jackie jaw drops.

Carrie's jaw drops. "Are you telling us that you, Andrew, Tierney and Alex are related to Brigitte? Are you telling us you are cousins?"

Tegan laughs and nods her head. "Distant, but yes."

"Have you always been close?"

"My dad, Seamus, was very close to Beatrice, but when she married I.A. that all changed. I.A. made a move on my mother and my father almost killed him. If it wasn't for Adrian Ayers I don't know what would have happened."

Carried can't stop laughing. "Wow, and we thought our family was interesting."

Tegan looks at Jackie and reaches out to her. "Tierney loves you, don't forget that."

Brigitte McCort was everything Tegan accused her of being and when she set her mind to something no one could change it. She believed what she wanted to believe and it didn't matter what Andrew told her she was sure Jackie was just like all the other college girls...out for one thing...to destroy Brigitte's family and there was no way she was ever going to allow that to happen again. Jackie's presence in their life triggered something alright, it triggered the all her insecurities.

Deciding she could not lose Andrew, not like she lost her father, she did the only thing she could think of. She tried to get rid of Jackie, tried to discredit her in Andrew's eyes and even went as far as to start rumors about her so she would be blacklisted from the hospital, but when nothing worked Brigitte contacted the one man who could eliminate the problem without care or concern for who he hurt or how he hurt them; she decided to call her father.

CHAPTER FIFTEEN

Brigitte was desperate to rid her life of Jackie Logan and she knew she needed help, but to call upon her father meant contacting a man she has not had any contact with since 1974. Hall had missed her high school graduation, missed her college graduation, he was absent from her wedding and never met her three children, his grandchildren.

Picking up the phone, Brigitte hesitates for a moment. "What am I doing?" she mumbles to herself. "What am I about to unleash? What will the cost be?"

Holding the phone in her hand, she takes a deep breath and then she exhales and sets the phone down.

"What if he doesn't accept my call? What if he wants nothing to do with me? What if..." she drops her eyes. "What if he tells me to go to hell?"

Sighing a heavy sigh, Brigitte reaches for the phone once again, looks at it and thinks about the rumor she's heard. The rumor that her father wants to run for the U.S. Senate.

"If that's true I might have a chance because he can't win without his family."

Dialing the only phone number she ever knew, she takes a deep breath and when it starts to ring her stomach clenches tight, her heart starts racing and she thinks she's going to throw up, but when the call goes to his voice mail this feeling of utter devastation washes over her. Taking a deep breath, she decides to take a chance, she decides to leave him a message.

Ending the call, Brigitte doubts she will ever hear back and for some reason the thought of that almost kills her, but she was about to be proven wrong.

Sitting in the rocking chair in her young son's room, she is rocking Ian to sleep when her phone rings at two o'clock in the morning.

Thinking it's Andrew, she reaches over to answer it. "Hello."

"Brigitte?"

Hearing his voice is like a punch in the gut. She had forgotten his sound, forgotten the slight Scottish accent and forgotten the way his voice made her feel. Suddenly everything came rushing back to her and for the first time in years she realized just how much she missed her father, but there was one problem...Brigitte's father was not the man she made him out to be. He was not the man she pictured in her mind. That man was never real, but the man who could eliminate Jackie Logan from her life was.

"Dad, I need your help."

I.A. listens to his daughter, hears the pain and panic in her voice and tells her he will be at her house first thing in the morning.

Surprised at his reaction, she puts her young son to bed and suddenly it hits her.

"Why is he so eager to help me?" she mumbles and walks out of Ian's room feeling unsettled and worries that she just opened Pandora's box upon her family. "Jesus, I think I just made a deal with the devil."

Walking to her room, she sits down on the edge of her bed and reaches for her phone to call Andrew. She needs to hear his voice, she needs him to come home, but when he answers the phone and she hears Jackie in the background she drops the receiver.

"Oh, my god, I have no choice. Jackie Logan is going to destroy my family."

Pulling back the covers, she climbs into bed and starts to cry when the phone rings, but this time she doesn't answer it, this time she ignores it and then she thinks about her father.

Jesus, what have I done?" she mumbles. "I.A. never does anything unless it benefits him."

The next morning, I.A. arrives, meets his grandchildren for the first time and talks to Brigitte who is convinced, more than ever, that Jackie Logan is going to destroy her family.

Seeing this as an opportunity, Ian Angus Hall promises he will take care of it and to prove it he places a call. "Anthony, I need you to take care of someone for me."

Brigitte's face falls, her heart sinks. *What is he doing? Who is Anthony? What did she just unleash?*

Thinking she is going to throw up, she starts to get up but I.A. stops her.

Shaking her head, she pulls her hand free. "Dad, this isn't want I meant, this isn't what I want, I wanted Jackie out of our lives...not dead."

He leans back on the couch, crosses his legs and unbuttons his suit jacket. "Well, you should have thought of that before you contacted me. You said you wanted her out of your life, you said she was going to destroy your family, you asked me to help, you summoned me here. I'm giving you what you want."

Thinking about that, she slowly lowers herself down on the chair and realizes what he's saying is true. "Oh, God, God forgive me," she whispers.

Ignoring his daughter's plea, he stands and walks over to the bar, pours himself a scotch. "Now that I've done this little favor for you, I need you to do something for me..."

Brigitte swallows. She knew her father had an evil side, she knew he was a bad guy, but she never expected this. "Dad, this was a mistake. I—

He holds up his hand. "It's done, Brigitte. Now it's your turn..."

"What?" she asks wiping her tears. "What do you want?"

"I want you to go to your mother and convince her to name you the new CEO of McCort-Hall Publishing."

"Why?"

I.A. sighs. "Let's just say, she betrayed me a long time ago and now that I have you back in my life it's time to make her pay."

Brigitte shakes her head. "What did she do?"

I.A. pours another scotch and shakes his head. "That doesn't matter right now. Once you become CEO I want you to offer Angus a job at the Chicago headquarters. Make sure his wife comes with him."

"Okay, but why?"

"I need you to keep an eye on him."

Brigitte looks at him.

I.A. drinks down his scotch. "After you do all that, I want you to give me a seat on the Board and I want you to put me on the payroll as a consultant at $12,000 per month."

Brigitte's jaw drops. "What? Why?"

He looks at her. "You know that story involving Lara Stuart?"

"The one about Lara Stuart and the human trafficking ring?"

"Yes."

Brigitte gasps. "Were you part of that?"

He looks at her and nods his head.

"But your name wasn't..." she looks at him and gasps. "Oh my god, what happened? What have you done? Are you being blackmailed?"

He nods his head. "Yes, $12,000 per month and if I go against the agreement he will release the information U.S. Attorney Peyton Logan, to Vice Admiral Paul Logan and to the press."

"What did you agree to?"

"It doesn't matter, but I had to make some promises and one of them was to leave Angus alone."

"Does Angus know the person who is blackmailing you?"

I.A. nods. "They went to college together."

"Were they..."

"Yes, his name is Daniel Donovan. If I interfere in Angus' life I will be in violation of the agreement, so you will need to do this for me. I want the senate seat and I can't get that with a gay son. I need you to keep Angus under control, I need to keep you all under my control."

"What if Mother or grandfather says no."

I.A. shakes his head. "She won't say no and as far as Adrian Ayers is concerned he won't interfere either," he says and reaches inside his coat pocket to pull out a sealed letter. "You show this to Beatrice and she will do exactly what you say."

"But dad..."

He looks at her as he walks to the back door. "Brigitte, you have no choice. You made a deal with the devil and signed it with your own blood. I just got rid of your problem now you need to get rid of mine."

August 4, 1989

Arriving at his twin brother's house at noon, Vice Admiral Paul Logan steps out of his fortified black SUV, steps between two armed guards and walks in as if he owns the place.

"Uncle Paul!" fourteen-year-old Olivia shouts and comes running toward him with her arms wide open.

"Uncle Paul!" Carrie shouts and walks in carrying her infant son on her hip while holding the hand of her two-year-old daughter, Laurie.

"Well, hello," he says and takes little Billy from her before he kisses everyone.

Peyton walks in and smiles as he dries his hands. "Paul!" he shouts and laughs. "Thought I needed to get in on it," he says and shrugs.

Laurie looks up at her grandfather and her great uncle. "Hey, you look the same."

Peyton squats down in front of her, scoops her up in his arms, and carries her over to his identical twin brother. "That's because Uncle Paul and I are twin brothers, identical twins."

She smiles and then she hugs Peyton, her grandfather, and squirms out of his arms to go back to her toys and play.

Paul looks at Peyton. "Is Jackie here yet?"

"Nope," Peyton says and takes Billy from Paul.

"Genevieve here?" Paul asks with a very different tone.

"Nope," Peyton says and then he laughs when he sees his brother's shoulders drop.

Peyton and Paul's brothers, Cal and Phillip, walk in next.

"Hey!" Cal shouts.

"Uncle Cal!" Olivia shouts and goes to him immediately to hug him.

"Uncle Phillip!" she shouts and turns to him as Carrie follows close behind.

Cal hugs everyone and then he looks at Paul. "Page and Frank are on their way. Is Jackie here yet?"

Peyton shakes his head. "Nope."

Cal looks at his younger brother. "Genevieve here?"

Peyton laughs, shakes his head and exhales. "Nope."

They all relax.

"Jesus," Peyton says and turns to look at Paul. "You are the Vice Admiral of the U.S. Navy, in charge of a special team's unit that answers only to the President and you're scared of my one-hundred-eight-pound wife?"

Paul kisses Billy's head. "I'm not afraid of Genevieve, I just don't like her."

Peyton exhales, but before he can reply he sees Genevieve pull into the driveway and right behind her is another car he does not recognize. "Who's that?" he asks out loud and then he walks out the front door.

"Shit, that's Jackie," Paul says and they all follow Peyton out.

Genevieve jumps out of her car and holds up her finger. "Jacqueline Elizabeth Logan, who is that?" she shouts. "Who drove you home?" Genevieve adds stomping toward her daughter. "And where is your car?" she shouts, walks up to Jackie and stops to look at her. "For God's sake, what are you wearing?"

Jackie looks at her father and her uncles, smiles and then she turns to face her mother. "Mother, I was in a car accident and a friend dropped me off. My car is at a shop and does it look like I'm naked?"

Genevieve's eyes widen. "No, but you are not dressed appropriately."

Peyton joins them, Jackie looks up, and smiles. "Hi, Daddy," she says and kisses her father's cheek.

"Hi, darling," Peyton says and kisses her back before he hugs her and passes Jackie off to Paul, who passes her to Cal and then onto Phillip, but just as she thinks she's done her uncles Page and Frank drive up and she hugs and kisses them, too.

"It's good to have you home, Beautiful," Uncle Paul sings and reaches for Jackie to hug her again. "How are you?" he asks and tries to get Jackie out of the line of fire, but Genevieve has other plans and when she steps up to Jackie Paul sighs as do all his brothers.

"Are you going to answer me, young lady?"

Jackie turns to face her mother. "Someone side swiped me on the highway as I was driving back to college from Lake Forest. They almost killed me."

Uncle Paul's jaw drops, Uncle Cal's does, too.

"When did this happen?" Peyton asks reaching out to check out his daughter.

Genevieve pushes Peyton out of the way. "Why didn't you call us?"

Jackie looks at her mother. "I didn't think you'd care."

Paul looks at Peyton and then to the other brothers.

"Fine, where is your car?" Genevieve asks.

Jackie looks up to the heavens, counts to ten, and then she looks at her mother. "Blake's dad took it, he brought one of his tow trucks and towed it back to St. Louis so he could fix it. Blake is supposed to deliver it back to me tomorrow morning."

"Oh," her mother says. "So, what about this outfit?"

Jackie looks at her mother, sighs, and then she steps forward. "Oh, mom, come on...this is what all the slutty girls are wearing these days. Don't you know?"

Her mother's jaw drops, but Jackie doesn't care. She's only going to be home for a few days and then she will return to school, start her Master's degree and if she can double down she will graduate in a year and move on.

August 6, 1989

Blake Thornton was Jackie's college boyfriend, he was the captain of the football team and the best Quarterback the university had seen in twenty years. He was so good, he was expected to be drafted by the NFL in January. Everyone knew he was destined for greatness, everyone knew he would go on to bigger and better things after graduation, but Blake didn't want any of that if he couldn't have it with Jackie.

Jackie Logan was the love of his life and even though Blake knew something was wrong when he visited her for Thanksgiving, he ignored it and when she told him there was someone else he wasn't surprised to hear it.

Not one to give up, Blake decided to give her some space and hoped she would come to her senses once Tierney left for Ireland, but he was wrong.

Blake saw the car accident as his last chance to change Jackie's mind and that's why he decided to deliver her car to her, but Anthony Leonetti had been watching Blake's father's body shop. Watching and waiting for Jackie to arrive and pick up her car, but he was getting tired of waiting and noticing a deli a block away he decided to take a walk. When he returned, Jackie's car was gone, the body shop was locked up for the night, and the shop manager was locking the big gates.

"Hey, what's going on?" Anthony asks.

"Closing time."

"There was a car, a white Ford, where did it go?"

The shop manager nods toward the car driving away. "Going home, I presume."

Anthony jumps into his car and without warning screeches off after the white Ford.

It was getting dark by the time he merged onto the highway, but Anthony was smart and he knew to keep his distance between him and the Ford until it was time to strike. Forty minutes later the traffic disappears and they are the only two cars on the road. Seeing this as the perfect opportunity Anthony makes his move, taps the side of Jackie's car, the driver swerves, he nudged it again and then he slams into the Ford, shoves it into the guardrail, and when he sees the sparks flying he makes his final move and the Ford disappear between the guardrail and an opening. Slamming on his breaks, Anthony jumps out and watches the car speed down the embankment, flip over several times and land upside down in the river below.

There was no one around when the accident happened, but Anthony knew it would only be a matter of time before someone saw the skid marks so he hopped into his car and took off.

Driving back toward the city, he pulls off at a gas station and makes the call. "It's done."

Sitting in the living room at her parents' home the next morning with her sister Olivia, Jackie wonders what is taking Blake so long. She wants to get going, she wants to get back to school, but when he doesn't arrive by noon she decides to wait on the porch swing.

"There you are," her Uncle Paul says and walks over to join her. "What are you doing out here?"

She looks up at him. "Blake is late, my mother is driving me crazy, and I want to get going. I need to get back to school."

"Ah." Paul says and nods his head. "So, what happened with Blake? Did you tell him about the other man in your life?"

Jackie shrugs. "Yes."

"How did it go?"

She shrugs again and looks away. "Fine."

"As simple as that?"

She shrugs again. "I don't want to talk about it."

"Okay, I respect that, but are you ever going to tell me about this guy?"

Jackie smiles. "He's pretty incredible, Carrie has met him so has Big Billy, Mary and Tom, and Theo and Sally. They really like him and he really likes them."

Her Uncle Paul nods. "I see..."

Jackie smiles. "He wants to marry me."

Paul's eyes light up. "Oh?"

She giggles. "Yeah, but I told him I needed a year or two. I want to finish my Master's degree in Nursing."

"What does he think about that?"

"He knows what I want and he supports it, but he doesn't seem to understand my desire to get it done *before* we get married."

Her Uncle Paul sighs. "You know, sweetheart, relationships require give and take, you can't always take. I think you need to learn how to compromise."

She smiles. "Acting a little too much like Genevieve, huh?"

He nods.

Jackie's eyes widen, but before she can say anything else two police cars pull up in front of her parents' house.

Peyton walks out to join them and sighs. "What now?" he says and thinking this has something to do with his job he walks down the steps to talk with the two state troopers.

"Good evening, Mr. Logan. We are sorry to bother you, but there's been an accident. Do you know where your daughter Jacqueline is?"

Peyton turns to look at Jackie. "She's on the front porch, why?"

The state troopers turn to look and follow him to the front porch as all Peyton's brothers walk out of the house to join them.

"Miss Logan," Trooper one says and extends his hand to her. "Do you own a 1982 Ford?"

"Yes, is there a problem?"

"Do you know where your car is?"

"My friend, Blake Thornton, is supposed to be delivering it to me this morning so I can get back to school, why?"

"Why does he have your car?"

Jackie looks at the officers and gives them a quizzical look. "Someone tried to run me off the highway four days ago, side swiped me as I was driving back to school from Lake Forest. Mr. Thornton owns a towing company and body shop. He brought one of his tow trucks and took it back to his shop to repair it. Blake offered to bring my car to me when it was finished being repaired. Has something happened?"

The officers look at one another. "Did you make a police report?"

Jackie nods her head. "Yes, hold on..." she says walks into the house to get the file folder and shows the officers pictures of the damage to her car as well as the police report.

"We will need to get a copy of that," Trooper two replies.

Peyton looks at the officers. "Okay, what is going on?"

The officers look at each other.

"We regret to inform you that Mr. Thornton was killed in a car accident late last night."

Jackie gasps and quickly covers her mouth.

Vice Admiral Paul Logan steps up to grab her and her father turns to look at the troopers. "Oh, my god, what happened?"

"According to the eyewitnesses parked next to the river, they heard a crash, heard screeching tires and then they saw sparks flying before the car drove off the highway, down the embankment and flipped over landing in the river. They said a man in an older model Cadillac convertible got out of his car and looked over the guardrail, waited a minute or two and then he—

Jackie gasps. "Hold on, is this the car?" she asks and holds up a picture of a 1976 El Dorado Convertible to show the officers.

"I believe so, why do you have a picture of it?"

"This is a picture of the same type of car that caused my accident."

Uncle Paul steps forward to look at all the pictures. "So, the same car was involved in both accidents?"

Peyton's jaw clenches tight.

"It looks that way," officer two states.

"Oh god," Jackie cries and starts to shake. "No...NO!" she shouts and collapses down into the arms of her father and sobs uncontrollably.

CHAPTER SIXTEEN

September 15, 1989

"Incoming!" Dr. Albers shouts as he runs past the nurse's station and out to meet the incoming ambulance. "Jackie, put the OR on standby. We'll triage and then send him up."

A worker from the Missouri Department of Transportation was hit by a truck while patching a series of pot holes along the highway. According to his co-workers, he was hit so hard his body was thrown more than thirty feet. He is in critical condition, his arm severed from his elbow.

The ambulance arrives and Dr. Albers jumps up into it to start evaluating the situation and Jackie joins him, but the smells of body odor, tar, dirt and grime are too much to bare in that small space and she must get out of there. Not knowing what is wrong, she starts to panic and everything starts spinning.

"Jackie!" Dr. Albers shouts when he sees her step back.

Jackie looks at him, she can hear him, she knows he is shouting orders at her, but she can't focus, she can't seem to get her footing and the smells are overwhelming her. Reaching for the side of the ambulance, she bends over to grab her knees, tries to take a deep breath but can't. Everything goes into slow motion, starts spinning and reaching up to rest the back of her hand against her forehead she closes her eyes for a second and the next thing she knows she is on the ground.

"ANNABETH!" Dr. Albers shouts. "Jackie collapsed, get a team out here!" he shouts and wheels the man with the severed arm past Jackie.

Jackie can hear her co-workers talking, shouting orders to get a pulse, to check her blood pressure and asking her friends if she's been sick. Jackie can feel everything they are doing to her, but they are jostling her around too much and suddenly she opens her eyes, rolls over on her side and throws up.

"Jesus!" Annabeth shouts grabbing a paper bucket to put under Jackie's mouth. "Jackie, what is going on?"

"I don't know," she mumbles and throws up again and again and again before she finally takes the towel to wipe her mouth. "Oh, god, I think I have the flu."

Dr. Elizabeth Anderson barges into Trauma Room Three and immediately starts checking Jackie's vitals when Jackie lunges forward, turns over on her side and vomits again.

"Jesus, what is that smell?" Jackie shouts and throws up again.

Dr. Anderson backs off. "Smell?" she repeats and looks around. "What smell?"

Jackie vomits again and tries to fight through it. "It smells like onions."

Dr. Anderson immediately reaches up to cover her mouth. "I just finished an Italian salad from Palmetto's..."

Jackie points. "Go, get out, the smell of the onions is..." she shouts and turns to vomit again, but this time nothing comes out. It's all dry heaves.

Dr. Anderson leaves and when she returns she has a mask over her mouth and Jackie can smell peppermint.

"All right," she says loudly. "Everyone out!" Dr. Anderson orders and within a matter of seconds all the nurses but one leave the room.

Dr. Anderson oversees all the Clinical Nursing Specialists in the Doctor of Nursing Program. She's the one who handpicked Jackie for the program.

"All right, Jackie," Dr. Anderson says and hands the bucket to the nurse who hands her a new one. "What is going on? Sue said you've been sick for about two maybe three weeks now."

Jackie looks up at her and then she bends over to throw up again, but nothing comes out.

Dr. Anderson rubs Jackie's back. "All right, all right," she sings. "Calm down."

Jackie sits up to try and catch her breath.

"Sue said you've been assessed for Influenza, she said they found nothing," Dr. Anderson says handing Jackie another towel and sits down next to her with a loud sigh. "Jackie, do you think you came back too early?" she asks with a change of tone and reaches up to tuck a loose strand of hair behind Jackie's ear. "I mean...Blake hasn't been gone that long. For god's sake, Jackie, you two had been dating for four years and he was killed in such a violent way..."

Jackie starts to cry.

Dr. Anderson tilts her head and her eyes fill with tears. "Jackie, we will understand if you need a little more time."

"No," Jackie says and wipes her tears before she blows her nose. "It's not that."

Dr. Anderson looks at her and sighs. "How can you be so sure?"

Jackie looks out the window and sees a group of small children playing on the playground outside the Trauma Center and starts to cry again.

"I broke up with Blake when I returned after my final Clinical at St. Matthew's Hospital."

Dr. Anderson sits up straighter. "Oh, I had no idea."

Jackie gets up to get rid of the paper bucket and rinses out her mouth. "I met someone when I was working at St. Matthew's," she confesses. "Someone incredible, Sheila."

Dr. Anderson shifts uncomfortably. "May I ask who?"

Jackie smiles. "You know Dr. Andrew McCort, right?"

Dr. Anderson's face falls.

Jackie laughs. "Don't worry it's not him."

Dr. Anderson releases the breath she's been holding. "Good, I know Andrew and I'm not sure I would have believed you."

"No, Andrew is a great man, he loves his wife and his family; besides, I could never do that," she says and shakes her head. "No, I'm talking about his brother, Tierney."

Dr. Anderson's eyes light up. "Oh, I know Tierney." Dr. Anderson says and Jackie watches a smile creep across her face. "He is one 'hot' McCort," she adds and gets up to walk over to a cabinet to pull out a box. "So, when was your last period?"

"End of July, early August."

Dr. Anderson starts to count on her fingers. "When was the last time you saw Tierney?"

"June," Jackie replies quickly and then she starts to cry harder.

"Oh."

Jackie shrugs. "Tierney went to Dublin; his father's construction company is building a new hospital and he needs to oversee the construction."

"I see...," she says and exhales.

Jackie looks up at Dr. Anderson and watches her reach for a plastic cup out of the cabinet.

"What are you doing?"

"Going on a hunch."

Jackie looks at her. "What happened to Blake was my fault. All of this is my fault. He was driving my car, whoever ran him off the road was trying to kill me."

"Jackie, who would want to kill you? This is not your fault."

"You don't understand!" Jackie shouts and jumps up off the bed. "I screwed up!" she cries and drops her head. "I was consumed with grief and I believed my mother when she said I caused it," she says and walks over to the window. "I've done something horrible. My mother was right about me."

"What did you do?"

Jackie can hardly talk. "After the memorial service, I was consumed with guilt. Tierney wanted to come home, but I told him not to. I felt like everything was my fault." Jackie says and wipes her tears away with the back of her hand. "I went to a bar, drank a hell of a lot of tequila and that's when Daniel Beringer showed up."

Dr. Anderson's eyes widen. "Daniel Beringer, the new adjunct professor for the School of Journalism? Hunky and smoking 'hot' Daniel Beringer?"

Jackie nods her head. "Yes," she says. "We started talking and Daniel helped me forget about Blake, Tierney, and my mother for a little while, but..." she narrows her eyes and rubs her forehead before she looks at Dr. Anderson. "I'm not sure what happened, but when I woke up the next morning. I woke up next to him, naked, and it was obvious we had sex."

Dr. Anderson grabs the box. "And when did this happen?"

Jackie shrugs. "The night of August 8th."

Dr. Anderson hands Jackie the box. "I need a urine sample."

Jackie slowly looks up at Dr. Anderson. "Oh god."

Dr. Anderson hands her a plastic cup. "Go," she says and nods toward the bathroom. "Fill it up."

Jackie gasps, her heart skips a beat, ice cold fear surges through her veins and as she walks across the room she knows this is her fate, her punishment for being promiscuous just like her mother warned. Stepping into the bathroom, this incredible ache in her chest continues to grow. Sitting down on the toilet, she places the cup between her legs and suddenly three things come to mind. One, her mother will disown her and ban her from their lives. Two, abortion is not an option. Three, her life, all her plans, Tierney, and all the things she ever wanted are about to be interrupted.

"Shit," she whispers, relieves herself into the small clear, plastic cup and looks at it for a few seconds before she stands to wash her hands. "What have I done?"

Standing next to Dr. Anderson, Jackie watches her take the plastic stick out of its wrapper and sets it down on the counter. Dipping the stick into the urine, Dr. Anderson quickly removes it and places it down on a paper towel. The waiting is excruciating, the results terrifying, and as the seconds' tick by the room starts spinning. Reaching out to rest her hand against the cool counter to steady herself, she realizes in less than a minute her life might change forever.

Staring at the stick the first blue line appear, it's almost instant and she can hear her breathing hitch, feel her pulse thump against the side of her neck and then another line appears and her breathing changes, she sounds winded, and in a matter of seconds the second line is just as obvious as the first and she covers her mouth before she bursts into tears.

Dr. Anderson immediately tries to comfort her, but Jackie can't allow it. Shaking her head, she turns on her heel and walks out. Ignoring everyone, not hearing a sound other than her own footsteps that match the sound of her beating heart. Reaching for her purse inside the locker, she turns and walks out of the clinic.

"This is my punishment, my cross to bear. Oh, my, god, my life is over," she whispers and as soon as she gets into her car she allows herself the nervous breakdown she deserves.

CHAPTER SEVENTEEN

Leaving the campus clinic Jackie has one thing on her mind, one person she wants to talk to and after talking to the Registrar's office she walks out with Daniel's address.

Walking up to the building, she pushes the button for the manager and waits.

An elderly woman walks out holding a tan cat and smiles. "May I help you?"

"I'm looking for Daniel Beringer."

The woman thinks for a moment and then she holds up a finger. "Oh, yes, the handsome man in 4D," she says and opens the door. "You are the second person to come by looking for him. Of course, I couldn't help the tall man with salt and pepper hair because he said he was looking for Daniel Donovan and I don't know a Daniel Donovan, but Daniel Beringer..." she mumbles and holds up her finger. "I know him."

Jackie smiles. "Do you know where he is?"

"Oh, honey, I'm sorry to tell you this but Daniel is gone. He's been called off on an assignment with the paper he works for. He left yesterday. Did he know you were coming?"

"No," Jackie mumbles.

"Oh," the apartment manager says dropping her head.

"I guess it was a long shot. It's just that I really need to speak with him."

The landlady sees the look on Jackie's face and holds up her finger. "Hold on, Daniel left me a note. He wants me to forward his mail to his mother. Let me see if he left me a phone number, too."

Jackie waits outside her apartment.

The woman returns holding a piece of paper. "Here you go, this is Daniel's mother's name, address, and phone number. I am supposed to call her when the movers get here and forward all his mail to her. If you'd like to copy it down, I'm sure that would be fine."

Jackie copies the information and hands it back. "Thank you," she mumbles, turns to leave and climbs back into her car to rest her hand on her belly. "Well, little one..." she says out loud. "Looks like we are about to meet your grandmother."

Arriving at the address on the paper, twenty miles west of St. Louis city, Jackie parks her car in the driveway of an elegant two-story home and gets out.

"Great, his mother has money. She's going to think that's all I want, but money has nothing to do with this."

Knocking on the double glass doors, Jackie waits.

A few moments later, a very pretty, short woman with dark brown hair and dark brown eyes opens the door. "Hello, may I help you?"

Jackie is caught off guard, this is not the woman she pictured as Daniel's mother when she was driving here. This woman looks like Sally Field.

"Um...hello," Jackie mumbles feeling guilty about what she is about to do. "My name is Jackie Logan and I'm looking for Daniel Beringer, do you know him?"

The woman standing at the front door smiles. "Yes, Daniel is my son, how may I help you?"

Jackie looks at her and starts to second guess herself.

The woman tilts her head. "Are you alright?"

Jackie blinks twice and without warning she starts to cry.

"Oh, my goodness, come in," Daniel's mother insists and reaches for Jackie's hand. "What is wrong?"

Standing in the foyer, not sure what to do, Jackie tries to gather her thoughts. "I...I need to talk to Daniel. Do you know how I can get hold of him?"

Daniel's mother shakes her head. "I'm sorry, sweetheart, Daniel is on assignment and I have no idea when I will hear from him."

Jackie nods and with a heavy sigh she turns to walk out when Daniel's mother stops her.

"Listen, I can see you are upset, would you like to tell me what is going on?"

Jackie looks at her. "I..."

Maria sees Jackie's reaction and decides on a different tactic. "Come on, if you don't want to tell me what is going on then let me pour you a glass of water or make you some hot tea," she says and takes Jackie's hand. "My name is Maria."

Jackie tries to smile, but fails miserably. "When Daniel goes off on assignment, how long is he gone?"

Maria exhales. "That's hard to say. He doesn't tell me where he is," she says and leads her into the largest kitchen she has ever seen.

"Who was at the front door, Maria?" a voice shouts from a room off the kitchen.

Maria rolls her eyes and turns toward the voice. "It's a young lady looking for Daniel, grandmother."

Jackie looks at Maria. "I think this was a mistake, I think I should go."

Maria reaches out to stop her when an elderly woman with salt and pepper hair walks out of a small bathroom and startles her.

"And who is this?" the woman asks with a strong Italian accent.

Jackie smiles and extends her hand. "Hello, my name is Jackie Logan, I'm a friend of Daniel's."

"Really?" the older woman asks and looks at Maria. "So, Daniel has lady friends?"

I glance over at Maria and she rolls her eyes.

The older lady walks past Jackie to sit down in a chair at the table. "Daniel isn't here, did you tell her that, Maria?"

"Yes, grandmother."

Jackie blushes.

The older woman looks at her. "So why are you still here? Daniel won't be coming home any time soon."

"Grandmother!"

"What?!" she shouts back at Maria. "I know how you are, darling. You hear Daniel's name and you want to help, but this girl is not here because she is in a relationship with Daniel, they are just friends so send her on her way," she says and gets up to open the oven to check on something.

The air suddenly fills with garlic, overwhelms Jackie and without warning she bends over and vomits all over the floor.

Maria gasps, the old lady turns to look and in less than a second Maria is running to Jackie with a trashcan.

"Oh, my god, she's pregnant..." the old lady says.

Maria looks up at her. "What?"

The old lady points. "She's pregnant, this girl is pregnant."

Jackie tries to make it stop, but she can't.

"BIRDIE!" Maria shouts. "Bring the mop and the bucket!"

Unable to vomit anymore, Jackie exhales and Maria hands her a kitchen towel.

"Oh, honey, are you alright?"

Jackie wipes her mouth and walks over to wash her face and hands in the sink as another woman walks in wearing a black dress and white apron, holding a mop and carrying a bucket.

Looking at her, Jackie holds up her hand. "Please let me clean this up. I'm so sorry, I'm so embarrassed."

"Don't be silly, we've got this," Maria says and rubs Jackie's back before leaving her to join Birdie.

"So, I'm right, aren't I?" the old lady asks moving over to Jackie. "You're pregnant and you are here to tell us my great grandson is the father."

Maria looks at Jackie. "Is that true?"

Jackie looks at Maria, turns to look at the old lady and then drops her eyes. "Yes."

Maria looks shocked, the old lady laughs and Birdie quickly takes the bucket and leaves.

"See," the old lady says. "Told you."

Maria stands there, her jaw on the floor and she looks like she is going to burst into tears as her grandmother walks by.

"And we thought Daniel was gay."

Jackie's eyes widen. "What?"

Maria snaps out of it and looks at her grandmother. "Well, we, um...Oh god."

Walking to the trashcan, Maria throws the paper towels she used to clean the floor into the bin and then she removes her gloves and throws those away as well.

Moving to stand in front of the sink, she washes her hands and with a shake of her head she turns to look at Jackie. "I'd be lying if I told you I'm not shocked to hear this. Daniel has never had a girlfriend and—

"Oh, I'm not his girlfriend. This pregnancy was not planned. I barely know Daniel."

The old lady returns. "What do you mean you barely know Daniel. If you barely know him then how did you get pregnant?" she asks and walks past her to get a soda out of the fridge.

Jackie looks at the old lady and then she looks at Maria. "I knew of Daniel, he's the talk of the university. Every girl wants to date him; every guy wants to hang out with him and the staff can't stop talking about him."

Maria tilts her head. "So, you never dated him?"

"No," Jackie admits.

"So how did this happen?"

Jackie exhales. "My college boyfriend was killed in a car accident after I broke up with him. I felt guilty, went to a bar, had too much tequila and Daniel walked in."

"And one thing led to another and..." the old lady shrugs and walks back to the kitchen table. "Come sit down," she insists and hands Jackie a cold soda.

Taking the can, Jackie sits down. "I didn't know what I was doing, I know it's not an excuse, but—

Maria joins them. "Does Daniel know who you are?"

Jackie nods. "Yes, he sought me out later the next day to see if I was alright and took me out to dinner. We talked and agreed to remain friends."

The old lady laughs. "You are a beautiful girl; how do you know Daniel is the father?"

Maria looks at Jackie.

Jackie narrows her eyes. "Daniel is the father and I will be happy to order a paternity test if he wants, but I know he is the father. I haven't been with anyone else in a long time."

Maria's eyes widen and then she begs Jackie's pardon. "Oh, no, honey, it's not that it's just..." Maria sighs.

The old lady takes a drink of her soda and sets the can down on the table. "It's like we said, we thought Daniel was gay."

Jackie shakes her head. "I don't know why you would think that. Daniels is a very attractive man and he has quite a reputation for being a lady's man."

Maria giggles and take the seat next to Jackie. "Really?"

Jackie laughs. "Yes."

The old lady takes another drink. "Or maybe you are just an incredibly beautiful woman and he couldn't help himself..." she mumbles and gets up to check on whatever is cooking in the large pot on the stove, adds a handful of spices and looks at Jackie and Maria. "He is still a man after all."

Maria sighs and shakes her head. "Ignore my grandmother and tell me what I can do? What do you want?"

Jackie shrugs. "I need to get hold of him, I need him to marry me."

Francesca chokes and Maria looks shocked.

"My grandson is not going to marry you because you are pregnant with his child. I would never allow it."

Jackie looks at her. "I'm not asking for a traditional marriage; I'm asking for a marriage in name only."

Maria jerks her head back. "Why?"

Jackie sighs. "My mother has very strong ideas and she believes a child born out of wedlock is a bastard child. If she finds out she will—

"Disown you..." Francesca interjects and suddenly has a change of heart and reaches for her hand. "I know all about that kind of mother," she says and looks at Maria.

Jackie starts to cry. "I don't want money from Daniel, I'll figure that out. I have a Bachelor's Degree in Nursing, I can get a job, I just need him to marry me."

"If you already have a degree, why were you at the university?"

"I'm in the Master's program," Jackie confesses and looks down. "I guess that's all over now..." she mumbles.

"Why do you say that?"

Jackie looks at her. "A child changes all that."

Francesca, Maria's grandmother leans forward. "You know you have choices."

Maria looks up at her grandmother and glares at her.

Jackie shakes her head. "I don't believe in abortion, and I won't even consider adoption. The thought of a child coming back to find me after eighteen years scares the hell out of me, so I guess I'm keeping it."

Maria looks at her and tilts her head. "Why do you say it like that?"

Jackie's eyes widen. "What do you mean?"

Francesca narrows her eyes. "If abortion is out of the question and adoption is not on the table, then why did you call the baby an 'it'?"

Jackie takes a deep breath and exhales. "I never wanted kids," she confesses. "I was not meant to be a mother; I don't think it's in my DNA."

"What about your mother?"

Jackie laughs. "My mother is crazy. She's a devout catholic, a strict disciplinarian, she didn't show love and she most definitely didn't love me. I have no idea what it means to be a mother."

Maria and Francesca look at each other.

Jackie nods. "My oldest brother, Peter, got a girl pregnant while in law school twelve years ago, and we haven't spoken to him or seen him since. My mother is an all or nothing kind of person and she will surely disown me. Not only that, but she will forbid my siblings and my great uncles to see me as well. Genevieve Logan is nothing if she's not stern," Jackie says and gets up to rinse out her finished can of soda. "My mother has never liked me; as a matter of fact, she has always hated me and now she will have her chance to get rid of me forever," she says her voice trailing off.

Maria looks at her grandmother and then she exhales. "So, you want Daniel to marry you in name only?"

Jackie nods.

"The only problem with that plan is we have no idea how long Daniel will be gone."

Jackie nods her head. "I understand," she says and stands. "May I ask you to do me a favor?"

Maria and Francesca stand.

"If Daniel calls," she starts and grabs a pen from her purse to write down her name and cell phone number. "Would you tell him I need to talk to him."

Maria takes the paper. "What are you going to do in the meantime? I mean, how far along are you?"

Jackie puts her pen away and zips up her purse. "I'm eight weeks."

"Then you will be showing soon," Maria says and starts to panic. "What will you do? Where will be? Can I keep in touch? I want to know my grandchild; I want to be part of this child's life. I can't just let you leave..."

Francesca looks at Maria and leaves.

Jackie reaches for Maria's hands. "I am going to apply for a nursing job a St. Matthew's hospital in the morning. It might take a few months, but as soon as I get enough saved to put a down payment on an apartment I will do that and let you know where I will be."

"And in the meantime?"

Jackie starts for the front door. "I'll check into a hotel near the hospital and take things one day at a time." Jackie says and walks to the front door. "Thank you for letting me into your home. It was nice to meet you."

"Hold on a moment!" Francesca shouts and joins them in the foyer, stops and speaks fluent Italian into her cell phone before turning to look at Jackie. "I need your bank's routing number and your account number."

Jackie's eyes widen. "What? Why?"

"Come on, I don't have all day." Francesca insists waving her hand at Jackie indicating she should hurry up.

Jackie reaches into her purse and hands Francesca her check book.

Francesca goes back to her call and Jackie looks at Maria.

Maria exhales. "I think you are staying for dinner."

Jackie's eyes widen and just like that she becomes part of Daniel's family and is led back to the kitchen to sit and watch Maria finish dinner.

CHAPTER EIGHTEEN

Maria Beringer and Francesca Leonetti are the most entertaining women Jackie has ever met and she can't help but like them. Partly because they are nothing like her mother, but mostly because they remind her of Bea, her Uncle Paul's "special friend" who Jackie has known since she was a toddler. Bea represents everything Jackie wants to be and she can't help but think Bea and Maria would be great friends.

Being with Maria and Francesca paints a different picture of Daniel and as Jackie learns more she begins to realize Daniel is a pretty good guy.

"So, tell me about Daniel, what kind of an assignment is he on?"

Kneading the dough to make pasta, Maria smiles. "The last big assignment he had was in the Middle East. He was reporting on the problems between Iraq and Iran."

Jackie's eyes widen. "Wow, what does Daniel do for a living?"

Maria looks at Francesca and then she tilts her head. "Don't you know?"

Jackie shakes her head. "No, it never came up."

Francesca laughs. "Daniel is an investigative reporter for The Sun," she says and shakes her head.

Jackie looks shocked. "Hold on, is Daniel...Daniel Donovan?"

They look at each other.

Jackie's eyes nearly pop out of head. "Oh, my god! No wonder you are so suspicious of me. Jesus, Daniel Beringer is Daniel Donovan?"

Maria nods her head. "Only four people know that, you are the fourth."

Jackie swallows. "Oh."

The front door opens and Maria leaves.

Francesca looks at Jackie. "Listen Jackie, there are some things you need to know about my family. Maria thought I was her mother most of her life, she didn't learn the man she thought was her brother was actually her father until she was in her twenties."

Jackie looks at her.

"It's a long story...my son Michael got a girl pregnant when he was fifteen, the girl's parents found out, sent her away and when I found out Michael and I found the girl and took the child after she was born."

"Maria?"

Francesca nods. "Yes."."

Jackie swallows.

"There is something else..." she says and nods toward Maria and a man standing at the front door. "Maria got pregnant when she was sixteen, married Daniel's father and we thought they were going to have a beautiful life, but fate intervened. Patrick was killed in a car accident on his way home to be here for Daniel's birth."

Jackie covers her mouth. "Oh, my god," she gasps. "So, Daniel never met knew his father?"

She shakes her head. "Daniel has had a rough time with this; I'm not sure how he will react to this little one, so I want you to be prepared."

"Okay," Jackie mumbles and looks at Maria standing at the door with a man. "Did Maria ever get married again?"

"Yes, she married Patrick's best friend, Ben Beringer."

"So, Maria's husband adopted Daniel?"

Francesca nods. "Ben Beringer was Patrick Donovan's best friend. They met at St. Louis College Prep..."

Jackie's eyes widen. "Really? My friend Tierney went to high school there."

"Great school," Francesca says.

Jackie nods her head. "So how old was Daniel when he found out?"

"He was seventeen." Francesca replies. "His high school English teacher assigned the boys to research their family's legacy. He wanted the boys to go back two to three generations, and they had to include personal stories which meant Daniel would have to do some research."

Francesca hands Jackie a bowl of pasta and adds more pasta to another bowl.

"The History Museum had a new genealogy room and Daniel couldn't wait to use it. He had never used Microfiche and couldn't wait to see what he could find. Deciding to look up his own birth certificate to get started he was surprised to find two documents instead of one. The first document he looked up was his original birth certificate, but it listed Patrick Daniel Donovan as his biological father not Benjamin Aaron Beringer and that piqued his interest.

The date, time, and location was correct, but his name was not. Instead of Daniel Patrick Beringer, born on July 4, 1955 at 7:10 AM it read Daniel Patrick Donovan."

"What did he do?"

"What any good investigative journalist would do, he looked up Patrick Daniel Donovan." Francesca says as if it was a stupid question.

Jackie laughs.

"Daniel found their marriage license, but when he discovered Maria had two he knew she was keeping a secret from him."

"Did he confront her?"

"Yes, that's when Maria told him what happened, told him Ben legally adopted him and then she told him about his biological father. It was quite a blow."

"I bet," Jackie says and sighs. "That's why I don't want to put the baby up for adoption. It's one thing for my life to be interrupted."

"Do you feel like your life is being interrupted?"

Jackie nods. "I was going to grad school and then I was going to apply to the Nurse Practitioner Program. I was going to marry the love of my life and now…" Jackie shakes her head and wipes her tears. "This baby changes all that, interrupts all my plans and it's my fault."

Francesca exhales.

"Did Daniel have a relationship with Patrick's family?"

Francesca bobs her head indicating yes and no. "They were there when he was born, but they kept their distance. They wanted to give Ben, Maria and Daniel a chance to become a family."

"Oh," Jackie says nodding her head. "So, Daniel uses the pen name Daniel Donovan in honor of his biological father."

"Yes," she mumbles but before she can say anything else Ben Beringer walks in with Maria.

Maria extends her hand toward Jackie. "Ben, this is Jackie Logan and Jackie is about to make us grandparents!"

Jackie stands to shake Ben's hand and he hugs her.

Several hours later, Jackie stands to leave and Ben walks her to her car.

"Now you listen to me, young lady," Ben says. "We will see to it that you get everything you need, but I don't think you should expect too much out of Daniel, nor do I think you should ever marry him. He is not hardwired to be a husband or a father," he says and then he looks back at the house. "But Maria...she deserves to be part of this child's life and she will love this child with all her heart."

Jackie drops her head. "I understand what you are saying, but I need Daniel to marry me otherwise I will be disowned by my family. My mother will see to it."

Ben sighs. "Maria told me, but when you consider what Daniel does for a living it might not be good for you or the baby."

Jackie looks away. "I never wanted this, I never wanted to be a mother and I'm terrified I'll screw up this child like my mother screwed me up, but it's more than that...I can't lose my sisters, my brothers, my father or my uncles I don't know what I would do."

Maria walks out to join them and hands Jackie a piece of paper. "I want you to go to the St. Andrew's Hotel in Lake Forest. I've reserved a suite in your name until we can figure things out and get you a real home."

"But..."

Maria nods her head toward Jackie's belly. "Now listen, this is my grandchild and I take care of my family. Call me tomorrow and let me know about the job. I want you to find a good OB/GYN and make an appointment. We'll go from there."

"Okay." Jackie mumbles. "Thank you."

Ben and Maria watch Jackie get into her car and close her door. "We'll talk tomorrow."

Jackie waves and then she drives to the St. Andrew's Hotel in Lake Forest, pulls up in front of the main entrance and handing over her keys to the valet she walks inside.

"Hi, my name is Jackie Logan and I—

The front desk clerk nods his head. "Yes, we've been waiting for your arrival. Here is your key," he says and hands Jackie an envelope with a card key. "Take the elevator on the left, it will take you to the tenth floor and use this card key to make entry into your suite. Our porter will bring your bags."

Jackie nods, does exactly what she was told and a few minutes later the elevator slows, the doors open and using her card key she opens the door to her suite. Walking into a small foyer, she gasps.

"Oh, my god."

Looking around she notices two doors on the left and opens them. One leads to a closet and the other leads to a half bath and to the right is a small kitchen that opens to the dining room and living room.

"Wow," mumbles.

Walking into the living room she notices a single door to the left, opens it to find a bedroom with a queen-sized bed and a private bath. Across the living is another set of doors, double doors, and walking over to check it out Jackie finds a much larger bedroom with a king-sized bed, a luxurious master bathroom and a large walk-in closet.

"Whoa."

Stepping toward the wall-to-wall curtains on the exterior wall, Jackie draws them back and her jaw drops.

"Holy cow, a balcony?" she mumbles and starts to walk out when she hears a knock at the door.

Turning to walk back inside, she lets the porter in and then she asks him if there is a restaurant nearby so she can get some dinner.

"Sure, but if you'd rather stay in you can always call room service. It's included with the suite. Just pick up the phone."

Jackie has never been in a place like this and she doubts she ever will be again, but while she waits for her dinner she thinks about Tierney, and missing him, she decides to give him a call.

Deciding honesty is the best policy, Jackie tells him what has happened, but his reaction is not what she expected. Instead of telling her it doesn't matter, he tells her he needs some time and suddenly her whole world starts to collapse around her, she's devastated and believes she has lost everything.

CHAPTER NINETEEN

Thinking her life will never be the same again, thinking she has lost the only man she has ever loved, Jackie goes to St. Matthew's Hospital first thing the next morning, hands in her resume and as she leaves HR she runs into Dr. Andrew McCort, Tierney's brother.

Already aware of Jackie's situation, hearing the news from Tierney, he seems relieved to see her at the hospital and even suggests she go see a friend of his, Dr. Susie McElroy.

"She's a fabulous OB/GYN, she's delivered all of my children and will deliver my next child as well."

Jackie looks at him. "Are you and Brigitte..."

He nods and smiles a big smile. "We're due April 25th."

Jackie giggles. "Congratulations. That's fantastic."

He exhales. "Yes...yes, it is."

"I'll give her a call and make an appointment, thank you."

Dr. Andrew nods his head and then he gives her another hug, tells her to give Tierney some time and then his beeper goes off and he leaves.

Feeling uncertain about her future, Jackie returns to the St. Andrew's Hotel and two days later she receives a call from the hospital offering her a job in the ER.

Three days after that she meets Dr. Susie McElroy, has her first ultrasound and visits the lab for bloodwork. Leaving, she has a picture of the peanut, knows her due date and has a prescription for prenatal vitamins.

Deciding to stay in for the night and celebrate with a pizza, Jackie calls Maria to tell her the good news.

"Oh honey, I'm so excited for you."

"Yeah, I'll be working with Dr. Andrew McCort again in the Trauma Center."

"And the baby?"

"My due date is April 30th."

"That's fantastic. I'm so happy. Maybe I can come with you to one of your appointments in the future."

Jackie thinks about that for a second and then she nods her head. "You know...I think I'd like that."

A week later she walks into her suite at the St. Andrew's Hotel, exhausted, feeling queasy, and reaches for the phone to order dinner when someone walks out of the half bath in the foyer and startles her.

Dropping the phone with wide eyes, she swallows. "Daniel?"

"Nice digs," he says and walks in wearing dark blue jeans and a polo shirt.

"Daniel, I..." Jackie can't believe her eyes. Not just because he is standing there in person, but because he looks really good.

Seeing her reaction, he tries to hide his smile but can't.

"What are you doing here?"

"I heard you needed to talk to me," he says and sits down. "My mother and grandmother seem to be quite smitten with you," he says and reaches for a bowl of peanuts.

Jackie sits down. "I...uh."

Putting his arm up on the back of the couch, he turns to face her. "So, I understand you're pregnant."

Her eyes widen.

"Am I the father?"

She nods her head.

He shakes his head, gets up to pour himself a glass of scotch and takes a drink. "I'll be damned," he mumbles and drinks down the rest of the amber liquid. "So, I guess I know why my mother insisted I had to come home so we could talk."

"I had no idea she got hold of you, she didn't tell me. I only asked her to have you call me."

Daniel looks at Jackie. "So, what do you want from me?"

Jackie starts to cry, tells him about her parents, about having to quit school and get a full-time job.

"Do you want this baby?"

She nods her head and then she shrugs. "I will not have an abortion if that's what you are asking and adoption is out, so I guess so...yes."

He looks at her. "Jackie, I'm not the marrying kind or the fatherly type. I don't want to have anything to do with either title."

She drops her head.

He sighs out loud. "Listen, how about a compromise...I will marry you, but it will be in name only so you can stay in good standing with your family. We'll go to the courthouse, have a quickie wedding and send the pictures to your parents, but I want you to keep your maiden name to keep you and the child safe."

Jackie can't believe it.

"But I need one thing from you," he says. "I want my mother and Ben to be part of this child's life. I mean it...my mother is the greatest woman I have ever known and she's been through a lot. I want her involved."

Jackie looks at him. "I like Maria...agreed."

He nods his head. "Okay, and as far as you quitting school goes...don't do that. Transfer to a program here in town, get your Master's degree and I'll take care of it," he says and pours another scotch.

"I don't know what to say," she mumbles and doesn't know what to say, but hugging him seems appropriate and then she starts to cry and the tears won't stop coming.

Three days later, on a Monday morning, they stand in front of a judge for a quickie wedding with Maria and Ben standing up for them and Francesca in attendance. When finished, they develop the pictures, mail them off to Jackie's parents and all her family members.

Several hours later, Jackie drives Daniel to the airport so he can return to his undercover assignment, but before he leaves he tosses her the keys to his Mercedes, tells her he will send money each month and kisses her cheek.

"Good luck, Jackie."

Jackie looks at Daniel with tears in her eyes. "Daniel, wait..." she cries and reaches for his arm. "Thank you for doing this, thank you for—

He leans back over and kisses her forehead. "It's okay. Just remember...my mother is a wonderful person with a big heart and I want her to be involved with this child."

"I know and I will, I promise."

Daniel smiles, caresses Jackie's cheek and sighs. "Remember what I told you, stay in school, and don't tell anyone I'm Daniel Donovan. There are bad people out there, Jackie. People who would hurt you, hurt this child, if they knew. Don't ever forget that."

She nods her head. "I won't. I won't even tell my family."

He sighs, tilts his head and leans in again to kiss her and this time it is a very different kiss, a toe-tingling kind of kiss and it leaves Jackie wondering if Daniel mean more to her than she thought.

CHAPTER TWENTY

Paul Logan has two lives. One shrouded in secrets, conspiracy theories and covert operations to protect the President and the country from corruption, domestic terrorism and treason and the other a secret white-picket fence kind of life with Bea and their girls. The problem...protecting one from the other.

Bea knows who Paul is, she knows what he does for a living, and she knows how dangerous it would be if anyone knew about her and the girls so she keeps his secret and goes to great lengths to make it possible for Paul to have both.

Arriving at Bea's beach house in Virginia Beach, Peyton pulls out the photos Jackie sent and shares them with Paul, but when he sees them he almost spits his beer all over him.

"Did you know about this?"

"No."

"What the hell, Peyton. This can't be. This can't happen. Jackie can't be married to Daniel Donovan. I won't allow it."

Peyton laughs, takes a beer from Bea and shakes his head. "Well, we don't have a say in it, it's already done."

Paul drops the pictures down on the table and walks outside to look out over the ocean on the back deck.

"Paul," Peyton mumbles, stepping out to join him. "Daniel doesn't know Jackie is my daughter if that's what you are thinking."

Paul takes another drink. "It isn't too late to get it annulled."

Peyton exhales and leans over the railing. "Actually, it is... Carrie sort of let it slip that Jackie had to get married..." he shrugs. "She's eight weeks pregnant."

"God dammit, Peyton!" Paul shouts and turns to look at him. "You know whose fault this is, you and I both do!"

Peyton sighs and looks away to take a drink of his beer. "I know...Genevieve."

Paul takes another drink and points his bottle at his twin brother. "This is your fault! You let her get away with that shit for too long and now look what's happened. Jackie's in danger, this child is in danger and none of this would have happened if Genevieve didn't have that god damn code of conduct or her twelve commandments," he spews and walks over to check on the hamburgers he put on the grill. "You and I both know Genevieve's ideas are crazy. I think she's crazy and I would NEVER have allowed Genevieve to tell me what to do. I would have NEVER abandoned Jackie; neither would Cal, Page, Phillip or Frank."

"I know," Peyton whispers and drops his head. "But what can I do? When Peter got that girl pregnant in Law School Genevieve almost had another nervous breakdown," he says and takes another drink. "Then Carrie got pregnant and she just..." he shakes his head.

"Peyton, your kids are not going to let Genevieve run their lives. When was the last time you saw Peter?"

"I haven't."

"Exactly!" Paul shouts. "Your kids know what they want and there is nothing Genevieve can say or do to stop them."

Peyton nods. "I know, but I also have to think about Genevieve's state of mind and she's not stable, Paul."

"I don't care!" Paul shouts. "Jackie would not have married Daniel if Genevieve wasn't always trying to control her."

Peyton exhales.

Paul leans up against the railing and looks at his twin brother. "I don't believe Jackie and Daniel have a real marriage."

"Neither do I," Peyton confesses.

Bea walks out to join them and hands Peyton another beer. "Are you two still worrying about Jackie?"

Paul nods. "Yes."

Bea sighs. "I'm sure Jackie can handle herself," she says and kisses Paul.

Paul narrows his eyes. "Remember that reporter who exposed the Lara Stuart Prostitution and human trafficking ring?"

"Daniel Donovan?"

Paul nods.

"Sure, I remember him, why?"

"Jackie married him and she's eight weeks pregnant."

"So, you think she had to marry him?"

Peyton sighs. "Yes, and if you think about the timeline Blake was killed a little more than eight weeks ago."

Paul looks at Peyton. "You're right. Dammit, you're right," he says and walks back to the grill to take the hamburgers off. "I bet they met at a bar, got drunk—

Paul shakes his head.

"It doesn't matter how it happened, all that matters is it did, and now we need to figure out a way to protect Jackie and the child."

Bea laughs. "Oh boy, Daniel better hope he never steps out of line or he will have you and your brothers to deal with."

Taking the platter, she takes the hamburgers inside with Paul and Peyton following close behind.

"Does Daniel know you are related to Jackie?" she asks and starts laughing. "I'm sure he doesn't. Jackie probably didn't say a word for fear he would run for the hills. I mean, you can't blame her for not telling him; she's in a lose-lose situation. Her father is a U.S. Attorney in charge of the criminal crimes division, she has an uncle who is a Vice Admiral in the U.S. Navy who just so happens to oversee a special unit of Homeland Security, another uncle who is the highest-ranking Judge at JAG Headquarters with over sixteen years on the bench, another uncle who is the Mayor of her hometown, another who works for the CDC and let's not forget about your youngest brother who is a Catholic priest!"

They both nod their heads in agreement when they hear someone walk in through the front door.

"PEYTON!" Major General Cal Logan shouts from inside the house.

Peyton looks up and groans. "Shit, they're here.

Major General Paschal "Cal" Logan walks in to the kitchen, sees his brothers and puts his hands on his hips. "What in the hell is going on? Why did Jackie get married at the courthouse and what is this about Jackie being pregnant?!"

Phillip Logan, the mayor of Ellie's hometown in southeast Missouri, steps in behind him and points. "You have some explaining to do! Why would Jackie do this and not invite us?"

Bea stops working on lunch and walks out of the kitchen with her hand up in the air. "I think I'll let you all talk, I need to attend to...well, I need to attend to anything else but this," she says and quickly walks up the stairs.

Peyton gives his brothers a dirty look. "I'm just as stunned as you are."

Cal walks over to him and pokes him in the chest with his finger. "This is Genevieve's fault!" he insists. "All that damn talk about code of conduct and her Twelve Commandments," he huffs and reaches for a beer from his brother Paul.

Phillip stands across from Peyton. "You should have put a stop to Genevieve's bullshit a long time ago, Peyton. For god's sake, you are a U.S. Attorney! Why don't you have control over your own wife?"

Peyton looks at him and then he takes a drink of his beer. "I know how it looks and I know you're right, but it's done."

Piaget Logan walks into the house with his youngest brother Frank and saying nothing he takes a beer from Paul, drinks down a big drink and then he sets down the beer. "Is this marriage real or did they do it to appease Genevieve?" he asks, looks around and when he sees the look on his brother's faces he shakes his head. "Stupid question, huh?"

"Yeah, stupid question, Page," Cal interjects, turns to look at Peyton and exhales. "What in the hell happened? One minute Jackie is in love with Blake, then there is this new guy, she's involved in a hit and run, Blake is killed driving her car, and now she married to and pregnant by a man she barely knows!"

"We know, Cal," Paul says.

Cal looks up and points to Paul. "Oh, and by the way, I have it on good authority that the man she married is Daniel Donovan, that investigative journalist from The Sun who just exposed that Human Trafficking Ring involving Lara Stuart!" he shouts and takes another drink. "What was Jackie thinking? How are we going to protect her?" he asks and looks up. "How are we going to protect the child?"

Paul sighs and holds up his hands. "Listen, I know we are all upset about this, and yes, Jackie married Daniel Donovan, but I'm more concerned about what he is investigating right now."

Cal slowly lowers his beer.

"Peyton and I think Daniel is investigating Damian Santos Delabro."

Cal, Phillip, Page and Frank freeze.

Peyton nods. "We think he is trying to infiltrate Delabro's network."

"Shit," Cal mutters. "If anyone finds out Jackie and Daniel are married she will become a target for sure."

Paul nods and then he looks at his brothers. "I talked to Jackie earlier, she said Daniel's biological grandfather bought her and the baby a house in Lake Forest across the street from St. Theresa's parish. He put it in her maiden name and even gave her enough money to buy furniture, bought her a car and created a trust fund for the baby's education."

Peyton turns to look at Paul. "Jesus, who is Daniel's biological grandfather?"

"I don't know, she didn't say, but knowing Jackie kept her maiden name makes me feel better," Paul says.

They all agree.

Peyton nods his head. "I agree and as long as Jackie keeps the house in her name no one will ever know she's married to Daniel."

"We can hope," Phillip interjects.

Paul looks at him. "Well, just in case we're wrong I can pull some strings and have Frank reassigned to St. Theresa's."

Fr. Frank Logan looks up.

Paul looks at him. "Frank could keep an eye on them, make sure they are safe and let us know if anything peculiar happens."

Bea returns in time to overhear Frank's new assignment. "You're moving to St. Theresa's? It wouldn't be St. Theresa's in Lake Forest, would it?"

Fr. Frank smiles. "Sounds like it, yes."

Bea gasps. "That's my daughter's home parish...

"Really?" Frank asks.

"St. Theresa's in Lake Forest?" Paul and Peyton say at the same time.

Bea laughs. "Yes, my daughter Brigitte belongs to St. Theresa's."

Peyton turns to look at Bea. "Isn't she the one who refuses to have anything to do with you because of Paul?"

Bea looks at Peyton. "Brigitte doesn't care about Paul or me for that matter. She only cares about her father."

"Who's her father?" Peyton asks.

"MOM!"

Bea jumps, looks inside the house and sees her daughter Katie and Katie's boyfriend Colin walk in.

"LOOK!" she shouts and holds up her left hand. "COLIN ASKED ME TO MARRY HIM!"

Everyone squeals and then they all go inside the house to open a bottle of champagne and celebrate.

CHAPTER TWENTY-ONE

April 28, 1990

Watching Jackie navigate the ER at eight and a half months pregnant, Dr. Andrew McCort is concerned. She looks tired and the closer she gets to her due date the more fatigued she is getting. Knowing Jackie is trying to juggle full-time school and part-time work he decides the time has come and orders her to go home.

"You are starting maternity leave early," he says and walks her to her car.

Jackie knows he's right, but she hates being alone and Maria can't be there all the time. Deciding she needs family, Jackie calls her sister Carrie and begs her to come stay for a few days even though Carrie is also eight months pregnant.

"Jackie..." Carrie cries. "Billy is not going to let me come up there for a few days, but I'll talk to him."

"Okay," Jackie mumbles when she hears someone at the front door. "Carrie, hold on."

Walking to the front door, she reaches for the handle and pulls the door toward her when she sees the one person she never expected to see ever again.

"Tierney?"

Tierney McCort looks up at her. "Hi."

Jackie immediately covers her mouth and bursts into tears.

Tierney steps up and under the small loggia, takes Jackie in his arms, and hugs her close. "I've been an idiot, please forgive me."

Jackie starts sobbing.

Leading her inside, he drops his bags and wraps both arms around her. "I don't care who the baby's father is, I love you and I want a life with you."

She looks up at him, and with tears swimming in her eyes, she suddenly reaches out to him, gasps and her water breaks. "Oh god!"

Stunned, Tierney looks at her for a second and then, without warning, he scoops her up in his arms and carries her out to his car, puts her in the passenger seat and buckles her in.

"Wait!" Jackie shouts. "I need my bag!"

Running into the house, he hears something, looks at the phone and grabs it. "Hello?"

"Tierney?"

"Carrie?"

"What's going on?"

"Jackie's water broke. I'm taking her to the hospital if I can find her bag," he cries looking around.

Shocked, Carrie tells him she is on her way.

"Hold on!" Tierney shouts. "What about the bag? Do you know where she put it?"

"Check the closet by the front door!"

Tierney does, sees it and ends the call.

Running out to his car, he reaches for his mobile phone and calls his brother Andrew at the hospital to tell him they are on their way.

April 30, 1990

Elizabeth Anne Beringer was born at 7:10AM weighing 7 pounds 2 ounces and measuring 19 inches long. She was the most popular baby in the nursery, all the nurses stopped by to see her, but it wasn't because she was Jackie's daughter it was because of her long, curly brown hair.

Calling her Ellie, Tierney thought she was the most beautiful baby he had ever seen and from the moment he cut her umbilical cord he was smitten. Ellie was perfect, she had a sweet disposition, loved to cuddle and barely made a peep unless she was stretching.

Everyone knew Tierney wasn't her biological father, but it was obvious Ellie touched his heart and even more obvious he loved her as if she was his own.

Watching Tierney with Ellie, Jackie can't help but sigh. Daniel wants nothing to do with the baby, he made that clear, but Maria was another story and Jackie wasn't sure how she would react to Tierney.

"Do you want me to call the baby's father?"

Jackie shakes her head. "No, he doesn't want to be involved. We got married because of my mother, it's in name only."

Tierney looks at Jackie. "What are you talking about?"

Jackie leans back. "My mother expects a certain level of conduct, she has her own set of commandments and if you break one she disowns you. My brother Peter got a girl pregnant while in law school, he didn't marry her, so Mother cut him out of her life and demanded we do the same."

Tierney looks at her. "Did you?"

"Of course not, but that doesn't mean Mother didn't. Peter is not allowed at my parents' house and she doesn't even recognize the child. I couldn't take that risk. I screwed up, you were gone, you weren't talking to me, and Daniel agreed to help me. We got married at the courthouse, he has taken care of me financially this whole time and he has taken care of school and everything. For a man who has no interest in being a husband or a father he has helped me out in more ways than I thought possible."

Tierney sits down in front of Jackie, still holding Ellie. "So, what is going to happen now that Ellie is here?"

"Daniel has no interest in being part of our life, but he did have one request...he wants his mother to be part of the baby's life."

Tierney nods. "Okay."

Maria walks in, sees Tierney holding Ellie and starts to cry.

Tierney immediately stands and hands the baby to her.

Maria looks down at the baby, tilts her head and wipes her tears. "Oh, Jackie, she's absolutely beautiful."

Jackie looks at Tierney before she looks at Maria. "Maria, I want you to meet Tierney McCort."

Maria looks at him. "I see..."

Tierney moves to sit down next to Jackie.

"Were you here when Jackie gave birth?"

"Yes," Tierney replies.

Maria looks down at Ellie. "Did Jackie tell you that her marriage to my son, Daniel, is in name only?"

Confused, Tierney looks at Jackie and nods his head. "Yes, yes Jackie told me."

Maria nods her head and walks over to the chair in the corner of the room to sit down. "Listen, I know Daniel wants nothing to do with this child and I am not going to try and tell you what to do, but I am not walking away from—

"NO!" Jackie and Tierney shout.

Jackie looks at Tierney and rests her hand on his leg. "Maria, I want you to be part of the baby's life, I want you to be part of my life, I want you here. Tierney just got back from Dublin, we have no idea what we want or what we are going to do, but that has nothing to do with you."

Tierney smiles at Maria. "Ellie likes you, she must know you are her Nanna."

Maria smiles. "I think you might be right."

He smiles and reaches out to touch Ellie's hair. "What do you think of all that hair?"

"Daniel had a lot of hair," she murmurs and runs her fingers through Ellie's curls. "I think she is the most beautiful baby I have ever seen."

Jackie smiles, but it doesn't quite reach her eyes and seeing her reaction worries Tierney. Most women are elated after giving birth, tired, but incredibly happy. Jackie is neither; as a matter of fact, she seems to be lost, distracted and confused.

Seeing the way Jackie shy's away from having anything to do with baby Ellie, Maria and Tierney take over and as the day drags on a steady stream of Logan's come to visit, pictures are taken and Ellie seems to touch everyone's heart.

Even Dr. Andrew McCort and his wife Brigitte come by for a visit with their family. Having just had a baby herself, Dr. Andrew wheels his wife into Jackie's room holding their new baby girl in her arms and introduces Jackie to baby Ava.

Jackie smiles, sits up and takes a good long look. "She's beautiful, Brigitte."

Brigitte smiles. "Thank you."

A strappy young man walks up to Jackie. "Hi, I'm Sean," he says and leans over his Uncle Tierney to look down at baby Ellie. "Wow, she has a lot of hair."

Jackie looks up at Dr. Andrew and smiles before looking back at Sean. "Yes, she does. How old are you?"

"Ten," he replies as his little sister steps up next to him and starts signing.

Jackie looks up at Dr. Andrew again, her boss, her friend and gives him a curious look.

Dr. Andrew smiles and starts signing to his daughter. "This is my friend, Jackie. She just had a baby like Mommy."

Caroline smiles and starts signing back as she speaks out loud. "What is the baby's name?"

Dr. Andrew looks at Jackie.

Jackie smiles. "The baby's name is Ellie."

Dr. Andrew signs the name to Caroline and Caroline smiles.

"She's beautiful," Caroline says. "I want to touch her hair."

Dr. Andrew takes her hand and gently puts it down on baby Ellie's head so she can touch her hair and Caroline smiles a big smile.

"My turn!" shouts another little one from behind Sean and pushes his way between his brother and sister.

Tierney's eyes light up. "Hey, little man," he says and they shake hands. "Jackie, this is Ian, Andrew's youngest son. He's three and he reads chapter books."

Jackie's eyes widen. "Really?"

Ian shrugs. "My mother says I'm gifted, it's not a big deal," he says and climbs up on the bed to sit next to Jackie and Tierney. "May I hold her?"

Dr. Andrew immediately shifts and moves to stand next to Ian when Jackie nods her head.

"Okay," Dr. Andrew says and reaches down to take Ellie from Tierney. "Ian, you must remember that newborns have soft spots on their heads."

Ian shifts to take a closer look and gently touches Ellie's head.

"You need to be very careful holding her and you need to make sure to hold her tight—

Tierney starts to reach over and his brother, Andrew, stops him.

"It's all right," he says and looks at three-year-old Ian. "Ian, do you understand what I mean by tight?"

Ian looks down at baby Ellie and smiles. "Yes, you actually mean secure."

Everyone looks at each other.

"Yes," Dr. Andrew says with a smirk. "Ready?" he asks and puts Ellie in Ian's arms.

The moment Ian and Ellie touch everyone hears a 'zap', look around and suddenly Ellie's eyes are wide open, Ian is staring down at her and everyone is mesmerized by the look on his face.

Brigitte looks at him. "Ian, are you all right?"

He continues to stare down at Ellie as Ellie looks up at him and then he smiles. "She's beautiful, she's my beautiful girl."

Everyone laughs.

Tierney reaches across to gently caress the side of Ellie's cheek and smiles at Ian. "You never know, Ian, Ellie might turn out to be the love of your life one day."

"She already is," Ian mumbles and everyone smirks. "She's so beautiful."

Jackie smiles and looks at Brigitte who has tears in her eyes and then she looks at Andrew who is looking down at Ian and Ellie with a big smile.

"Why don't we take some pictures," Tierney says and hands his camera off to his twin sister, Tegan, who just walked in.

As all the McCort's and Logan's arrive, they can't stop oohing and ahhing over Baby Ellie and keeping a watchful eye on Jackie, Tierney's concern continues to grow.

Moving back to Jackie, Tierney sits down next to her and kisses her cheek. "Hey, maybe Ava and Ellie will grow up to be best friends."

Brigitte starts to cry; no one knows why. "I think we should get going."

Everyone seems startled by Brigitte's strange reaction, but that is quickly forgotten when Genevieve Logan arrives and suddenly the tension is so thick you can cut it with a knife.

CHAPTER TWENTY-TWO

Genevieve Logan walks in like she owns the place, sets down her purse, removes her white gloves and grabs Ellie out of little Ian McCort's arms, looks at her and sighs as if disappointed.

"She looks like you, Jacqueline."

Jackie swallows.

Tierney quickly escorts his brother and Brigitte out and then he returns.

Genevieve looks over at him, looks at Maria and then she looks straight at Jackie. "And who is this?"

Jackie looks at Tierney and her eyes widen. "Um...this is my friend Tierney. He was there when I went into labor."

Genevieve glances over at Maria. "And where is Daniel?"

Maria slowly gets up and takes baby Ellie. "Daniel is still on assignment."

Genevieve threads her fingers together. "And have you told him that his child was born?"

Maria looks at her. "Of course, I have. I sent him a message."

Genevieve nods her head and looks at her daughter. "I don't know what is really going on here, but if you think I will stand by and allow you to commit adultery you have another thing coming," she says without emotion.

Jackie's siblings exhale, her uncles all stand with wide eyes and both Tierney and Maria have no idea what to say.

Fixing her dress, standing up straighter, Genevieve turns to face Peyton. "We are leaving."

Jackie reaches out to her. "Mother, no, you don't understand."

Genevieve jerks as if possessed and puts her finger in Jackie's face. "Divorce is not an option," she says sternly. "You made your bed and now you have to lie in it. You can't simply get a divorce because Daniel is not a good husband. I'm sure you understood that before you married him," she adds.

Jackie's face blushes the color of a ripe tomato and she drops her eyes. "Of course, I understood that Mother."

Maria's eyes widen, Tierney's eyes widen, and Tegan looks terrified.

Genevieve bends over to grab her purse. "I will not tolerate you disrespecting your marriage vows and if I find out you are lying to me you will not be welcome in my home ever again and neither will your bastard child...you decide."

Peyton and Paul exchange glances and then Peyton quickly grabs Genevieve's arm and leads her out, but it's too late. Jackie immediately drops her head and starts sobbing, Tierney doesn't know what to do and Maria looks like she is going to burst into tears any second. Thinking fast, Paul moves to sit by Jackie, takes her in his arms and kisses the side of her head.

"I'm sorry, sweetheart, I'm so sorry."

Jackie turns to him and everyone decides maybe it's time to give Jackie a moment with her uncle and leave.

Reaching up to grab her face between his hands, Paul looks down at her swollen eyes and kisses her forehead. "What is really going on?"

Jackie sniffs, wipes her nose and drops her eyes. "I broke up with Blake because of Tierney," she whispers. "Tierney was away on business when Blake was killed, I felt like his death was my fault. I went to a bar after the Memorial Service and got drunk, ran into Daniel, and then I found out I was pregnant," she mumbles and shrugs.

Paul exhales and pulls her up against his chest to hug her. "Oh, honey."

"I wish Ellie was Tierney's, I wish that more than anything in the world."

"So, I was right about your marriage, it's in name only, isn't it?"

She nods. "Daniel didn't want me to lose my family, but—

Paul immediately pushes her back and grabs her face again. "You are never going to lose your family; we all know how Genevieve is and no one cares what she thinks. She's insane, Jackie, and the only reason Peyton puts up with it is he doesn't want a repeat of what happened right after you were born."

She furrows her eyebrows and pulls back to look at him. "What are you talking about?"

He sighs, closes his eyes and rests his forehead against Jackie's forehead. "Genevieve had a nervous breakdown right after giving birth to you, it was really bad, she had to be institutionalized for almost a year."

Jackie's eyes widen.

"When she was finally well enough to come home, the doctors made it clear to Peyton that she should never get pregnant again, even suggested she have her tubes tied, but Genevieve refused. She saw herself as a vessel for God's will. She got pregnant with Carrie right away and slipped right into another depression, it was awful, she was horrible to deal with, and Peyton was a mess. He didn't know what to do, so he took her back to the institution and our Mother took over caring for you and all your siblings."

"What about Carrie?"

Paul blinks. "She was born in the institution."

"I never knew this."

Paul sighs. "I know, your father wanted to keep it a secret, but secrets have a way of coming out when you least expect it."

Maria and Tierney come back in.

Maria moves over to stand next to Jackie, sees the look of sadness in her eyes and exhales as she turns to face Paul. "Paul, Daniel wants nothing to do with being a husband or a father, and Tierney is a good man," she says and reaches over to squeeze Tierney's hand. "I'm okay with Tierney being in Ellie's life," she says and looks at Tierney.

Tierney looks at her. "Are you sure?"

Maria nods and wipes her tears. "Yes."

Paul nods and sighs a heavy sigh. "Well, then, that settles it," he says and stands with his hands on his hips. "If you want to continue keeping this relationship a secret from your mother that is your choice," he says and stands. "Just remember...there are two types of secrets: the kind you want to keep hidden, and the kind you don't dare let out."

CHAPTER TWENTY-THREE

May 15, 2004

U.S. Attorney Peyton Logan is preparing to present his case to the federal grand jury when his secretary walks in.

"Congressman Ira Weismann is on the phone for you."

Peyton's eyes widen and he grabs the phone. "U.S. Attorney Peyton Logan."

"Peyton, Ira Weismann. I'm ready to talk to you, but you have to guarantee immunity or I say nothing and take it to my grave."

Peyton looks at his assistant. "Where do you want to meet?"

"The St. Andrew's Hotel in Charleston."

Twenty-four hours later Congressman Ira Weismann walks into the private dining room looking terrified and weary.

Placing a recording device on the table, Peyton nods to Megan, his assistant, to transcribe the entire conversation.

"I was hoping we could get a drink first and order some dinner," Weismann says, his hands shaking.

Seeing the state of mind Ira is in Peyton agrees. "Fine," he says and calls for their waiter.

It's all very normal, but what they are about to talk about is anything but.

Ira takes a drink from his martini to calm his nerves and hands Peyton a manila envelope.

"What's this?"

"Something you need to see."

Peyton opens the envelope and sees pictures of Jackie tied to a bed, blindfolded and her mouth is duct taped.

Peyton is shocked. "Where did you get these?"

"It doesn't matter. You know it's true, you know it happened and if you don't back off from this federal grand jury the same thing will happen to your daughter Carrie."

"What?"

"Look, Peyton, the person who sent this wants one thing. They want you to stop and if you don't. Not only will they go after your daughter Carrie, but they will release those pictures to the media, humiliate your entire family and suggest a story that involves you going on a witch hunt to find the men who did that to her," he says and reaches for his drink. "It's enough to plant reasonable doubt."

"Hall is behind this, isn't he?"

"That's why I'm here," Ira says and sets his drink down. "We need to talk."

Peyton swallows. "You son of a bitch, did you do this to my daughter?!"

Ira leans forward. "Peyton, you need to stop this witch hunt. Nabbing I.A. is not worth putting your family at risk. He's too powerful and he won't stop until you do."

Peyton puts the pictures away.

Ira gives Peyton a sympathetic look. "Listen, Peyton, there is another way to get what you want..."

Peyton looks at Ira. "What do you mean? What are you talking about?"

Ira leans forward. "I'm being blackmailed."

Peyton narrows his eyes.

"Why are you being blackmailed?" Peyton asks.

"I was on the yacht Glory Be that fateful weekend back in the late 80's. I purchased the services of young women for sex and I should have been arrested, but Hall got tipped off and called for a helicopter when we were thirty miles from shore."

Peyton leans forward. "Who tipped him off? Who is blackmailing you?"

"I don't know who tipped him off, but Daniel Donovan is blackmailing us."

Peyton's eyes widen.

Weismann doesn't see it, he's too engrossed in his gin to notice. "Donovan didn't like that we got off the yacht before the bust, he wanted us to pay for what we did, and he knew I.A. would never stop unless he did something to stop him."

"So, he blackmailed all of you?"

"I guess Daniel thought we would pressure I.A. into doing the right thing, but I.A. could care less what we have to say."

"Was this your first time attending and participating in an event like that?"

"No."

Peyton looks up. "How many times have you attended an event like the one on the Glory Be?"

Ira raises his hands and shrugs. "The first time was in 1969, mostly college girls, and then four times a year ever since, so do the math."

"Were you an active participant every time?"

"Yes."

"How many purchases did you make at each event?"

He tilts his head back and thinks for a second. "Six to ten."

Peyton's eyes widen. "Why are you telling me this?"

"I've been diagnosed with testicular cancer; I don't know how long I have to live and I want to die with a clean conscience. Indict me if you have to indict anyone. Throw the book at me; I deserve it."

Peyton rubs his chin. "Who introduced you to it?"

"Hall," he says quickly.

"What else do you know?"

"I know I.A. hates you."

"And why is that?"

Ira rubs his jaw. "Because he knows you are about to destroy his political career and blow up his life."

Peyton narrows his eyes.

"He knows you are calling a grand jury, he knows you are about to bring him up on charges of corruption, racketeering and fraud, he knows you know about the shares in B&M Pharmaceuticals, he knows you know about the Glory Be and he knows you have more on him…"

"Good."

"I figured you'd say that, but Peyton…I.A. will never stop until he silences you for good and seeing what he did to your daughter I want you to think about this," Ira replies in a flippant tone.

Peyton tries not to react. "Are you the only one being blackmailed?"

Ira leans forward. "No."

Peyton can't believe this. "What were Daniel's demands?"

"Money and the protection of Angus Hall."

Peyton's hands start to sweat. "Angus? Why does Daniel care about Angus?"

"I don't know."

Peyton stands and looks at Ira. "All this information is well and good, but it's not going to change my mind."

Ira sighs. "Well, you can't say I didn't try."

"Why did you really come here?"

"I want to die with a clear conscience."

"Is that all?"

"No, I was hoping you'd heed my warning. If you go in front of the grand jury I.A. will go after another member of your family and he won't stop until you do."

Peyton says nothing.

Walking out of the hotel, Peyton and his assistant Megan climb into a black SUV and their driver rushes them to the airport.

Once inside, Peyton reaches for a phone to call his brother. "Paul, I need you to send your guys to the hospital. No, I'll explain later. I need you to put Jackie and the kids under protective custody, and send more guys to the rest of my family," he says sounding upset.

"Peyton, what is going on?"

"I know who attacked Jackie, and if I go in front of the grand jury they are going after Carrie next."

"Jesus."

"I'm going back to the hotel, putting Genevieve on a plane and driving to D.C. to convene a grand jury. I need you to protect my family."

"Call me when you get to D.C., I'll take care of the rest."

Peyton looks at Megan. "Megan, send Paul a copy of everything that happened at that meeting."

Refusing to allow Peyton to drive to D.C. on his own, Genevieve climbs into the passenger seat and tells him she is going with him.

Not up for an argument, Peyton climbs into the driver's seat, starts the engine and takes off for D.C., but Peyton and Genevieve never make it.

CHAPTER TWENTY-FOUR

"There are no secrets that time won't reveal."

- Jean Racine

September 6, 1995

"Elizabeth Anne Beringer, it is three o'clock in the morning, what are you doing?"

Little five-year-old Ellie looks up. "I'm making breakfast."

Jackie looks around, sees the pancake mix, milk, eggs, and oil. "Ellie, it is not time for breakfast," she cries and notices Ellie is already wearing her uniform, her pretty little socks and her new dark brown Mary Jane's. "Why are you in your uniform?"

Ellie looks up and smiles. "Today is my first day of kindergarten."

Jackie takes the whisk from her daughter and sets it down in the bowl, removes the Little Chef apron Maria bought Ellie for her birthday and then she gasps.

"Ellie, your uniform!"

"Sorry."

Jackie puts her hands on her hips and looks at her daughter. "Listen, Ellie, I know you're excited about going to school, I know how much this means to you, but now I have to wash your uniform again and—

Ellie drops her head.

Jackie sees it, takes a deep breath and exhales. "Ellie..."

Ellie looks up at her mother. "I just wanted to go to school."

Jackie reaches down to caress her daughter's cheek. "I know," she mumbles and looks at the island. "I'll tell you what...you take off that uniform so I can wash it again, go back to bed for a few more hours and I'll make you the best blueberry pancakes you've ever had."

Ellie smiles. "Really?"

Jackie smiles and helps Ellie take off her uniform. "There we go."

Ellie hugs her mother, something she has never done and it catches Jackie off guard. Reaching down, she pats Ellie's back, squats down and hugs her back.

Ellie leans back and looks at her mother.

Jackie isn't sure what to do, they've never had a moment like this, so she does the only thing she can think of. Standing, she reaches for Ellie's hand.

"Okay, time for sleep."

Ellie nods her head and then she skips up the steps.

Putting Nicholas into the stroller, Jackie turns to check on Ellie and sees her packing her lunch box. Deciding she'd better check on this, she sneaks into the kitchen to see what her daughter is doing.

Seeing a baggie full of carrots, a cup of ranch dressing, a bag of pretzels, a fruit cup, and an apple juice box, Jackie can't help but giggle. "Do you think you have enough snacks?"

Ellie looks at her and starts to cry.

"Oh, no, honey, I didn't mean..." Jackie turns Ellie around to hug her. "Why are you crying?"

Ellie looks down. "I want to be like all the kids."

Jackie looks back at the stroller, looks at Ellie and then she looks out the back door at her white Honda. "Did you want me to drive you to school?"

Ellie nods.

Jackie tilts her head. "You want to be like all the other kids?"

Ellie nods.

Jackie smiles, hugs her daughter for the second time and stands. "Well, if we are going to drive to school, we'll need to get your brother in his car seat. Do you want to help?"

Ellie smiles.

Driving around the back side of St. Theresa's catholic church, past the rectory and the playground behind the school, they continue past all the houses to the stop sign and Jackie signals to make a right.

Pulling up behind all the other moms and dads lined up in front of them to drop off their kids, Ellie sits in the backseat and tries not to giggle out loud.

Pulling up to the 'Student Drop Off' sign, Jackie stops and unlocks all the doors when a very handsome young man with dark brown wavy hair and Caribbean blue eyes walks up to the car and opens the back door wearing a light blue polo shirt and navy blue pants with a bright orange safety vest over his clothes.

"Hi, Jackie."

"Hi, Ian."

Ian looks down at Ellie, reaches across her and unbuckles her seatbelt. "Are you ready for your first day of kindergarten, Beautiful?"

Ellie smiles.

Ian smiles.

Reaching out to take her little hand, she slides it into his and suddenly there is a loud 'zap' that lights up between them, a bright silver light that 'snaps' like a firecracker and they both look down in awe.

Jackie leans back. "Are you okay?"

Ian looks at Ellie, Ellie looks up at Ian, and they both smile.

"Yes, we're fine," Ian says.

Jackie sees the way Ian looks at Ellie and smiles. "Hey, Ian, I understand you have a birthday coming up soon. How old will you be?"

Ian smiles. "Nine."

"Nine?" Jackie asks sounding a little shocked. "But you're in sixth grade, aren't you?"

Ian turns to look at her. "Yeah, I skipped a few grades."

"I guess so..."

Jackie leaves and Ian walks Ellie to her classroom, helps her hang up her new pink backpack with butterflies on the back and then he takes her hand to show her where her spot is at the table.

"Okay," Ian mumbles playing with her long curly hair. "I guess I should go back. Will you be all right?"

Ellie looks up at him and smiles. "I'll be all right."

Ian starts to walk away, but when he sees Ellie take a book to the carpet he changes his mind.

"You know...I think I can stay a little longer. Would you like me to read that book to you?"

Ellie shakes her head. "No, I can read it."

Ian laughs. "You can?"

Ellie nods her head.

"Show me," Ian insists and sits down next to her and pulls her over to sit on his lap.

Ellie reads the title and then she opens the book. "In the light of the—

Ian's eyes widen, he can't believe his ears. Ellie is reading to him, she is reading with perfect fluency and she even changes her tone of voice when the story changes. When she's finished, he hands her another book, a chapter book, and she reads a chapter to him.

"Wow," he says sounding shocked. "How about this one..." he says and hands her a thick book. "This is a book about a young girl who gets into lots of trouble..."

Ellie smiles. "I know, I've been reading the series all summer. My Nanna and I go to the library every Saturday."

Ian's eyes nearly pop out of his head. "You know, I started reading books like this when I was in kindergarten, too."

Ellie laughs. "You did?"

Ian nods. "Uh-huh."

Ellie giggles and gets up to get another book when a spunky little blond comes hopping into the kindergarten classroom, sees Ian and puts her hands on her hips.

"Ian McCort! Where were you? You told me you'd be there when Daddy dropped me off and you weren't there!"

Ian blushes, gets up to walk to her and grabs her shoulder. "Ava, chill out!"

A tall man with short strawberry blond hair and brown eyes walks in and tilts his head. "Ian, your sister refused to walk in with anyone else but you so I had to park my car and walk her in myself. Where were you?"

Ellie walks back to the carpet and sits down to read another book and Ian watches her open it, set it down on her lap and lean over to read it.

Dr. Andrew looks around Ian, smiles and reaches out. "Ellie?"

Ellie looks up, sees Dr. Andrew and puts her book to the side. "Dr. Andrew!"

Dr. Andrew McCort bends over, holds out his arms and hugs Ellie. "Hello, sweetheart. Happy first day of school!"

Ellie giggles.

Ava looks at her father and gasps. "Daddy, what are you doing?"

He looks at her. "I'm hugging Ellie."

Ava pushes her father back. "Who is Ellie?"

Dr. Andrew smiles, grabs Ava to hug her and still squatting he introduces his youngest daughter to Ellie. "Ava McCort, this is Ellie Beringer. I work with her mom at the hospital."

"Is your mom a doctor like my father?"

Ellie shakes her head. "No, she's a nurse."

"Oh," she says and reaches for Ellie's hand to walk with her to the cubbies. "My Daddy says the nurses make him look good, does your Mom make my Daddy look good?"

Ellie shrugs.

Dr. Andrew looks at Mrs. Smith, the kindergarten teacher, and smiles. "We never know what she's going to say."

Ellie's first day at St. Theresa's wasn't just her first day at school, it was the day she met her first friend and it was the day she met the first and only boy she would ever love.

CHAPTER TWENTY-FIVE

Ian McCort had no idea Ellie Beringer would grow up to be the love of his life, but there was something about her, something he couldn't deny. He wanted to be with her, he wanted to protect her, he needed to keep her safe, and he hated being away from her.

Ellie felt the same way.

As they grew older, their feelings for each other continued to grow, but Ian was too old for Ellie, he knew it and so did she. They tried to fight it, they tried to resist it, but when Ellie turned thirteen all that changed.

Ellie didn't look like a little girl anymore, she looked like a beautiful teenage girl and everyone noticed; especially Ian, but he kept his distance, distracted himself as much as he could, and refused to allow himself to think about her like that until one night it all became too much.

They were at a Memorial Day pool party, Ellie was wearing a little string bikini and within minutes of arriving she was surrounded by young studs. When Ian arrived with all his friends, he noticed what was going on and he didn't like it.

His friends knew it was only a matter of time, they knew how he felt about her, and they suspected she felt the same. Keeping an eye on her, everything was fine until one of the young studs untied her bikini top and that's when Ian snapped.

No one could have predicted what would happen next, but it changed their lives forever and sent them down a path neither one of them wanted.

Taking Ellie home, a big storm hit the St. Louis area and Ian decided to stay, but when the power went out and both Ellie and her younger brother panicked he decided to stay. Walking in through the back door after working a double shift, Jackie caught

Ian and Ellie asleep on the couch together and knew she had to do something or Ellie could end up like her.

"Ian, Ellie is too young for you, what were you thinking?"

"Jackie, I can't stay away from her. I don't know why but I can't," he cried and paced the kitchen. "I'm in love with her."

"Ian," Jackie exhales. "You are almost seventeen years old, you are going off to medical school some five hundred miles away, and you are three and a half years older than Ellie. This won't work, it can't work out, she's too young!" she demands and holds up her hands. "Your dad and I have noticed the way you look at Ellie, we see the way she looks at you and we agree that this cannot and should not happen.

"But—

Jackie holds up her hand. "No! I will not allow it. Ellie is thirteen years old, she has her whole life ahead of her and I will not allow you to ruin her life."

"I won't ruin her life."

Jackie looks out the window over the sink. "Yes, you will. Ellie will end up like me and she will resent you for it."

Ian shakes his head. "What are you talking about?"

Jackie turns to look at him. "It doesn't matter. I will not let you interrupt my daughter's life. She needs time to grow up, time to figure herself out and you need to go to college, do the things college boys do, date lots of girls and—

Ian's jaw drops. "But I don't want to do that."

"Yes, you do."

Ian exhales, leans up against the base cabinets and crosses his arms and ankles. "You don't understand, Jackie."

Jackie looks at him, sees the look on his face and sighs. "I'll tell you what...you stay away from Ellie until she is seventeen, give her time to grow up and spread her wings, if you still feel like this in four years I'll allow you to date her, but that doesn't mean sex. I want Ellie to graduate from high school, go to college and have a better life than I did. I won't let you take that from her."

"Fine, but I can't stay away. I need to see her, I need to know she's safe, and I need to protect her."

Jackie looks at him. "Ian, I can see how much Ellie means to you, but she's just too young."

"What if I promise not to tell Ellie how I feel or make a move on her until she is seventeen."

Jackie looks at him and exhales. "Eighteen and I'll let you see her as long as Ava or Nick is around."

With a nod of his head, Ian promises to wait until Ellie's eighteenth birthday, but keeping that promise would prove to be very difficult; especially after he moved in with her and Nick after her seventeenth birthday.

May 16, 2008

Bzzz. Bzzz. Bzzz.

Ellie reaches up from a sound sleep and taps her alarm. "It's too early..." she groans and flips over on her belly to go back to sleep.

Bzzz. Bzzz. Bzzz.

Smiling, Ian rolls over Ellie and reaches for her alarm to turn it off, kisses her cheek and looks up at the picture of him holding her in his arms the day she was born.

Today is the day and knowing it he leans down to rest his lips against her ear. "Good morning, Beautiful," he whispers and kisses Ellie below her left ear.

"Mmm," she moans. "When did you get home?"

"Four," he whispers and slides his hand under her t-shirt to rub her back. "I'll tell you what...why don't you stay in bed and I'll get Nick ready for school, walk him over to St. Theresa's and then I'll come back and join you again."

"Mmm," she moans and when she feels him shift to get out of bed she opens her eyes. "Wait! What?" she asks and rolls over on her side to face him. "Have you slept?"

He smiles that glorious deep dimple smile. "Nope, I've been watching you sleep."

Ellie laughs, covers her face and groans. "I hate it when you do that."

He pulls on his button-fly jeans and looks at her. "Go back to sleep, Beautiful. I'll be back," he says and bends over to kiss her.

Propping her head up against the palm of her hand, Ellie watches him sit down on the edge of the bed to put on his tennis shoes and wonders what is going on. Ian's different. He's more affectionate, more loving, and more attentive, all things he shied away from in the past.

"I don't know what is going on with you, but I like it," Ellie mumbles and watches him put on one of his college t-shirts.

Ian looks down at her, runs his fingers through her hair and caresses her cheek. "I'm glad you like it, I like it, too, and I finally feel like myself again," he says and leans over to kiss her, lingers and leans in again to deepen the kiss until he hears Nick in the hall and pulls back. "I'll be back," he says, winks and leaves.

Smiling a big smile, she rolls over on her back and giggles. "What is going on?" she asks, covers her face and giggles. Moving her hands down to rest over her heart she sighs. "Is he finally ready?" she asks and looks over at the picture of them taken on the Logan family's annual float trip. "What is it about turning eighteen, what changed?"

Lying back, she closes her eyes and thinks about all the times she tried to kiss him and he pulled back, thinks about all the times she tried to be affectionate and he'd find an excuse to stop it before it went too far, and then she thinks about all the times he rejected her and all the times she slept on the couch rather than be humiliated again.

"What is going on?" she mumbles and leans back to close her eyes.

Unaware of how much time has passed, Ellie feels Ian climb back into bed with her and rolls over to face him and snuggle up against him thinking he will push her away, but when he doesn't she immediately opens her eyes.

"Hi," he whispers.

"Hi,"

He leans down to kiss her and all her muscles clench tight, and when she responds by pushing her right thing between his and kisses him back she is surprised that he doesn't stop her.

"I want you," he whispers against her ear and trails kisses down her neck.

"What?" she asks panting hard.

He moves back to her mouth and rolls over on top of her, reaches for her hands and pulls them up and over her head. "I want you," he whispers again.

Ellie pulls back to look at him. "Ian."

He sits up and takes her with him, reaches for the hem of her shirt and lifts it up and over her head.

She swallows. "Ian, what are you doing?" she asks quickly covering herself.

He looks down at her, reaches for her hands and pulls them down to look at her. "Something I've been wanting to do for five years."

She laughs and blushes bright red. "Oh really?"

Looking down at her, he slides his hands up her body and touches her breasts, fondles them and then he smiles and looking into her eyes he pushes her back and leans down between her breasts, kisses her chest and looks at her. "Really."

Glancing over at her clock she sees the time and gasps. "Oh, my god, is it 8:30?"

He puts her right beast into his mouth and swirls his tongue around her nipple and it feels so different, it feels so good, she isn't sure what to do. "Oh god!" she cries and squirms under him.

With a sexy smile on his face, he pulls back and looks at her. "I'm perfectly aware of what time it is," he murmurs and leans down to kiss her left breast.

Ellie's whole body reacts and she isn't sure what to do with all this sensation, it's too much.

Pulling back a second time, he moves back to her mouth and this time his kisses are anything but soft.

Moaning out loud, she wraps her arms around him, slides her hands up and down his naked back and kisses him back.

"You are so beautiful," he murmurs. "I love you so much."

Sitting up, Ellie pushes him back. "Ian, what is going on?"

He looks at her. "You aren't seventeen anymore, there are no more promises to keep..." he mumbles and leans back down to kiss her again.

Reaching up to push him back, she looks at him. "What promises? What are you talking about?"

He shakes his head. "Nothing," he whispers and pulls her forward to sit on his lap. "I love you and I want you," he whispers and kisses her again.

Reaching up to wrap her arms around him, she can't believe what she just heard him say and when she finally gives in and kisses him back everything explodes between them.

"Oh god," she cries feeling his mammoth sized erection between her legs. "Is this finally happening?" she mumbles and drops her head back so he can kiss her neck.

"I—

His phone starts buzzing and she immediately pushes him back.

He looks at her, shocked by her reaction, and reaches over for his phone, makes a strange face and taps the screen.

"Mother..."

Ellie quickly scoots off him and jumps out of bed covering herself with his t-shirt.

He looks up at her and makes a face as he continues his conversation with his mother. "Oh yeah, great...No, I'm still in bed," he says and smiles at Ellie as she takes a step back. "No, I'll come over and pick it up," he promises and grabs Ellie's hand to pull her back to him. "I don't know," he mumbles and leans down to kiss her. "Maybe an hour."

"Ian, stop," Ellie whispers and tries to pull free but he won't let her. "Stop."

He laughs and lunges for again, but she shakes her head and opens the bedroom door.

He covers his phone. "Hey, where are you going?"

Ellie looks over her shoulder, drops his t-shirt and tosses it at him. "I'm going to take a shower."

He shakes his head and watches her skip to the bathroom. "No, mother, I'm still here," he says.

Ellie looks back at him and then she disappears from his view.

"What the hell was that?" she asks stepping into the shower. "All these years he pushed me away, all these years he barely touched me, and now..."

Stepping under the showerhead she soaks her hair and reaches for the shampoo when she hears the bathroom door open and close, hears the shower curtain open and then she feels Ian's hands on her.

"Ian!" she shouts and quickly covers herself. "What are you doing?"

"Taking a shower with you."

Turning to look at him she gasps and for the first time in her life Ellie Beringer sees Ian McCort completely naked.

Reaching for the shampoo, he squirts some into the palm of his hand and reaches up to wash her hair. "And now I'm washing your hair," he says in a sexy, sultry voice, he kisses her. "When I'm finished, I'm going to wash your body and then I think I'm going to—

"ELLIE!" someone shouts from the first floor. "Where are you? I'm here to take you to school!" she sings.

Ellie's heart skips a beat. "Shit! It's my mother!"

Ian laughs and continues washing her hair.

"Ian."

"What?" he asks and starts laughing. "Tell your mother you just got in the shower, tell her to wait downstairs; tell her you'll be right down."

Ellie does as she's told and then Ian does what he said he was going to do and after he washes her hair he washes her body and as he does he kisses every inch of her.

"Have you had breakfast yet?" Jackie Logan asks shouting up the stairs.

Ellie jumps and pushes Ian back in reaction.

"Tell her 'no'."

"NO!" Ellie shouts and her voice cracks because she is so nervous she thinks she is going to pass out.

"Okay!" she shouts back. "If you hurry up I can take you to get something to eat, too."

Ellie looks at Ian and see the disappointed look on his face. This is not going as planned.

Standing, he grabs her chin, tilts her head back and kisses her. "I need to get you out of town or I'll never get any time alone with you."

Ellie smiles and wraps her arms around his neck. "You want to spend some time alone with me?"

"I do," he whispers. "I want to take you away for a couple weeks, I want to be alone with you, take you to see beautiful places and buy you beautiful things, but mostly I want to make love to you."

Ellie can't believe it, but when she starts to say something the door to the bathroom opens, startles them both, and Ellie immediately moves to protect Ian, and pops her head out.

"Elizabeth Anne Beringer, come on! I need to get you to school," Jackie says and hands her two towels. "Is Ian still picking you up after practice?"

"Yes," Ellie says making sure to block Ian and steps out wearing a towel around her head and another around her body while making sure to keep the curtain closed.

"Lou is driving me crazy and his kids are making me nuts. I had to get out of there, that's why I'm early."

"Oh, uh-huh, let's go to my room so I can get dressed."

They leave and Ian gets out of the shower as he hears Jackie ask if Ellie is ever going to put her closet door back on and then she goes on and on about her third husband, Lou and Lou's kids.

"...and I thought Daniel was a pain in my ass...I should have never married Lou either."

Ellie rolls her eyes and quickly changes into a pair of dark blue ankle length skinny jeans with a cute light blue sleeveless top that has pierced embroidery across the front and a scalloped hem. Reaching for the new denim colored high heeled crystal embellished sandals Ian bought her for her birthday with the glittery sole, she smiles and puts them on.

"Whoa, cute shoes," Jackie says and smiles. "Ian?"

Nodding her head, Ellie pulls her hair back at the top, fastens it with a barrette and lets her caramel colored long curls hang down her back.

"Has Ian talked to you today?"

Ellie turns away from her mother to put on a little makeup and then she reaches for her purse and grabs her sunglasses. "Um...yes, I've talked to him, why?"

Jackie shrugs. "I was just curious."

Ellie walks out of her bedroom, looks at the bathroom door and as she walks by a wave of crushing disappointment washes over her. She has waited her whole life for Ian, saved herself for him and she knows what she wants. Ellie wants him.

Walking down the stairs, she can't help but wonder what is going on, why Ian is being so affectionate and forthcoming, but when she rounds the corner to walk into the kitchen she gets the biggest shock of her life.

"Ian!" her mother shouts. "I didn't know you were stopping by this morning?"

Ian smiles, moves to hug Jackie and kisses her cheek. "I just left the gym and wanted to see my girl before I went home."

Blushing bright red, Ellie bites her lip.

With a big smile on his face he reaches out to hug Ellie. "Hi."

"Hi."

He kisses her cheek and leans in against her ear. "Don't worry, we have our whole lives ahead of us."

Jackie watches them and sighs. "Do you want to take Ellie to school?"

Ian smirks. "No, I have a few errands to run..." he says and reaches for Ellie's chin to tilt her head back and kisses her. "But I'll be there to pick you up."

"Maybe I should drive myself. Aren't you on call?" Ellie asks.

He smiles. "Nope. I took today off," he says and slides his hand down her backside to grab her bottom.

She gasps and blushes bright red.

He watches her reaction and kisses her again. "I also took off the entire weekend, and the next two weeks."

Ellie tilts her head. "I don't believe you."

He smiles and leans down to kiss her. "It's true," he says.

Jackie giggles.

"I took off to spend some time with you," he says and grabs her chin to tilt her head back. "...stop worrying. The hospital is not going to call."

Jackie giggles. "I think I'll give you two a moment."

Ian looks at her and then he looks back at Ellie.

Ellie looks up at him and slides her hands around his waist. "So, if you are off..." she mumbles. "...and I'm off..."

He laughs. "You aren't off yet."

She smiles and bites her lip. "You're right."

He looks up at the clock. "What time do you need to be at school to rehearse the graduation ceremony?"

"9:30."

She looks up and gasps. "Mom! We need to go!"

Leaning back against the counter, he takes a drink from his coffee and clears his throat. "Um...love those shoes."

Ellie looks over her left shoulder and giggles. "You should, you bought them for me."

He smiles a big smile and nods his head. "I have great taste."

Ellie smiles. "Yeah, you do."

Three hours later Merici Academy is wrapping up the girls' graduation practice when Joan Hart walks over to talk with Ellie.

"So some of the girls are going out for lunch, do you want to join us?"

Ellie crosses her arms. "No, thank you. I already have plans."

Seeing the ring on Ellie's left ring finger, Joan grabs her hand. "When did you get that?"

Ellie looks down and smiles. "For my birthday."

"Is there a reason half of the infinity symbol is diamonds and the other half are sapphires?"

"Yes."

Joan waits.

"I—

Suddenly every girl turns to look at something and Ellie smiles. She can sense him before she sees him and when she turns to look in the same direction she sees his blue convertible Porsche pull into the circle drive, park and feels butterflies swarm her belly.

Watching him get out of his convertible, she bites her lip and rests her hand over her belly as she watches him walk toward her wearing those sexy button-fly faded blue jeans, those tan leather shoes and a blue polo shirt with those aviator sunglasses.

Another girl walks up to them. "Jesus, who is that?"

Ellie smiles. "That is Ian McCort, Doctor Ian McCort...my boyfriend."

Joan's eyes widen. "No, he's not. That's not true!"

Several others join them and gasp.

"So, Ian's real? He really does exist?"

Ellie giggles and nods her head. "Of course, he exists," she says smiling at him. "He's a surgical resident at the children's hospital near Lake Forest," she mumbles and walks over to meet him.

"Hi, Beautiful," Ian says and grabs Ellie to hug her and then he kisses her. "Are you finished?"

Ellie smiles and even though she can barely articulate a full sentence she nods her head and he smiles that glorious smile of his.

One of the girls looks at Joan. "Looks like you're wrong. He sure looks like he's with Ellie to me."

Joan exhales, crosses her arms and makes a sour face.

"Let's go," he says and takes her hand, threads his fingers through hers and starts to lead her away when he does something completely unexpected. Stopping, he wraps his arms around her and kisses her in front of Ellie's entire graduating class. "How about some lunch?"

Sitting across from each other at lunch, Ian reaches for her hand with a serious look on his face and just as he is about to say something his cell phone buzzes, he looks down and the look on his face changes instantly.

"Dr. McCort."

Ellie's face falls.

"Ian, we need you to come in."

"What?"

"Dr. Wu got sick and we have a heart on the way from Utah. We need you to scrub in with the heart transplant team."

Ian's face falls. "Are you kidding me?"

"No, we need you here as soon as possible."

Speechless, Ian looks at Ellie and she immediately stands.

"Sounds like we need to get you back to the hospital."

He ends the call and stands. "But I don't want to go. I want to stay with you, I want to spend the night with you and..."

Ellie looks at him and put her hands on her hips. "Ian, this is a big deal. They have never called you in for something like this. You need to do it."

"Yeah, but I'm off the schedule and..." he grabs her when he sees her shake her head. "No, Ellie. I want to stay with you."

"I'll be here when you get back and didn't you say you had the whole weekend off? The next two weeks off?"

He nods his head slowly.

"Ian, this is a big deal for your career. I want you to be happy."

He slides his hands around her and pulls her closer. "You make me happy," he murmurs and his phone starts buzzing again.

"Go, I want you to go."

"Are you sure?" he asks, covering the mouthpiece of his phone.

She nods.

He tells the Chief of Surgery he needs to take Ellie home and then he'll be on his way.

Driving up to Ellie's house, he reaches for her hand and kisses it. "I love you, Ellie."

Her eyes widen. "You do?"

He smiles.

Ellie starts to cry. "I love you, too." she whispers, leans over to kiss him, and then she gets out of his car.

"I'll see you in a couple hours."

"Okay," she says and closes the door.

Ian leaves and as he does this old black Cadillac convertible turns the corner by St. Theresa's church and catches her eye, but before she can turn to get a good look at the driver her brother Nick opens the front door.

"Ellie!" Nick shouts and holds up the cordless phone. "You have a phone call! It's Grandpa Ben!"

Running into the house, Ellie takes the phone. "Hello."

"Ellie, it's Grandpa Ben."

"Oh, hi."

"Listen, sweetheart, I hate to call you so late in the afternoon, but I need your help."

"Oh?"

"Well, you see, the judge agreed to an early release for Daniel so he could help Nanna and I get her to chemotherapy and cardiac rehab, but he seems to have disappeared and my buddy, Hank, just informed me that three Spanish speaking men were in his pub earlier today looking for Daniel. I'm worried those bad guys know he was released and, well, I have a bad feeling that's all."

"What can I do?"

"Would you mind driving out here, I'll pay for your gas. I need help finding him. He can't be too far away."

Ellie looks at Nick. "Let me drop Nick off at his friend's house for a party and then I'll be out."

"Okay, sweetheart, let me know when you are close."

Grabbing her cellphone and her purse, she tries to call Ian but the call drops, calls him back and the second time she gets a strange recording that his phone is not accepting calls at this time, and when she tries to send him a text it won't go through.

"What is going on?"

Not sure what else to do, she decides to leave him a note on the refrigerator, grabs her keys and leaves.

Epilogue

May 16, 2008, 8AM

Walking down the stairs to start her day, Brigitte McCort sees a man standing at her front door and walks over to see what he wants.

"Hello, may I help you?"

"Yes, I have a delivery from Al Amoudi Jewelers for Ian McCort."

Brigitte tilts her head. "He's not here right now, but I'll be happy to accept it."

The driver hesitates and takes out his phone to place a call, but no one answers.

Watching the man's reaction, Brigitte sighs. "Listen, I'm his mother. I'm sure he won't mind."

The driver relents. "Okay, please sign here."

Brigitte signs for the package and then she starts for the kitchen when she hears someone else at the front door and turns to walk back.

"Yes, may I help you?"

"Delivery for Ian McCort," he says hands her the envelope and she signs for it.

"What's this?" she asks and looks down at the flat envelope.

The man shrugs. "Don't know," he says and leaves.

Taking the packages into the kitchen she sets them down on the granite counter top and looks at them. Reaching out to pick up the first package, she shakes it and then she laughs and reaches for the second to check out the return address and when she sees that it is from a U.S. Government Agency she quickly covers her mouth.

"Oh god!" she gasps. "Ian is going to propose to Ellie."

Reaching for the house phone, Brigitte quickly calls her father.

"Hello."

"Dad, I need to see you."

"Why?"

"Ian is going to propose to Ellie!"

"What?"

Brigitte is frantic now, pacing the kitchen and getting more upset by the minute. "It's true. I know it is. Two packages arrived at the house this morning. One from Al Amoudi Jewelers and one from a U.S. Government Agency. I think one is a ring and the other is a passport," she says. "Oh, and by the way, Ian has Mother's jet on standby. I think he is taking Ellie on a trip to propose!"

"Okay, calm down."

"Dad! Don't you know what this means? If Ian proposes to Ellie then he won't be free to marry Victoria and—

"All right, all right. I'll take care of it."

"What are you going to do?"

He exhales. "What you've always wanted me to do."

"Oh, Dad, I don't know..."

"Brigitte, this is the only option. We need to get rid of this girl once and for all and unless you can think of another way I'm running out of options."

"I..."

I.A. exhales. "That's what I thought."

"Dad, Ellie is the same age as Ava..." she whispers.

"It's done, Brigitte. I don't want to hear another word about it. I'm sick of it. You are finally going to get what you want," he says sounding final. Now...we have another problem."

"What?"

"Daniel Donovan has been released from prison."

"Oh god."

"Yes, and as you can see I have more important things to worry about," he says and ends the call.

With his phone in his hand, he makes a call to Lara Stuart.

"Hello."

"Lara, I need you to get hold of Anthony; I have a job for him."

"What sort of a job?"

"Brigitte just called...Ian is taking that girl on a trip and Brigitte thinks he is going to propose."

Lara sighs. "I.A., what are you doing? Brigitte is paranoid. I think you should let this go."

"Let me worry about that. Tell Anthony I want it done and I want it done tonight. Call Flynn, tell him to make sure Ian is at the hospital so Anthony can get to her."

"I.A.—

"Lara!" I.A. shouts. "If I wanted your opinion, I'd ask for it. Now do as I say!" he shouts.

"Fine," she hisses.

"One more thing...I need you to contact Delabro and tell him Daniel has been released from prison."

"What? When did that happen?"

"This morning. My source tells me his mother petitioned the courts for an early release. She has stage four cancer and his father just had a heart attack. They need his help. He is on his way to their house as we speak. If we are going to take him out, now is the perfect time. I want to end this situation once and for all."

"What about his threat to release the information?"

"I've already taken care of Peyton, if I have to take care of Paul I will. I have no other choice; I need to stop Daniel."

"I.A. do you realize what you are saying?"

"Yes, but I don't have a choice. Delabro made it clear it is either me or Daniel. I'd rather it be Daniel."

Lara Stuart exhales. "I think you are making a big mistake. I think you need to think about this. If Daniel releases his evidence, you'll have more than Paul Logan to worry about."

"Call him. Tell Delabro to send his assassins. I want this done tonight."

May 16 2008, 5PM

Sitting at his desk overlooking Constitution Avenue, newly appointed Senator I.A. Hall is looking over the agenda for his evening meeting when his personal cell phone rings.

"Hall," he says distractedly.

"Dad, have you heard anything?"

He looks up immediately. "Brigitte?" he asks as if not expecting to hear from her. "No, I have not heard anything," he says turning his attention back to the agenda.

"Maybe it isn't too late to stop this."

He sighs. "Brigitte, it's not like this is the first time you've done this. Do I need to remind you about that nurse nineteen years ago? You remember, the one you were sure was having an affair with Andrew?"

She is quiet for several seconds and then he hears her whimper.

"Maybe I was wrong, maybe Ian isn't as involved with this girl as I thought."

I.A. groans. "Brigitte, you were the one who insisted we put a stop to this relationship. You were sure he was taking the girl out of the country and even more convinced he was going to propose marriage. If that's true we have to stop them. I need Ian to marry Victoria VonMeister, I need her shares in B&M Pharmaceuticals, you know that, it's always been part of the plan. This girl could ruin everything. What's up with the sudden change of heart?" he asks sounding aggravated.

"It's just that she is so young and—

"For god's sake, Brigitte, you've been trying to get this girl out of Ian's life for five years, you've gone to great lengths to do so, even at a personal loss, so what's going on?"

She sighs a heavy sigh. "You're right. Ellie will ruin everything for us, all our plans for Ian, everything," she says sounding nervous. "It's just that, I don't know, she's eighteen years old and..."

I.A. smirks. "Sounds like your conscience is bothering you."

Brigitte sighs.

"Brigitte you've threatened the girl, you threatened Ian, you drugged her and tried to make it so he caught her with someone else. You have even gone as far as finding a look-alike to try and trick him," he says and exhales. "You've been more ruthless than me. I mean, come on, you even played the family card, insisted he go to Maui over Christmas Break, and invited Victoria to join him in his bed..."

"Stop!" she insists. "I know what I've done, Dad."

"Brigitte, Ian left Maui, he took a commercial flight to Denver, rented a truck and drove back to her on Christmas Eve. Sean went with him, Andrew, Caroline, and Ava followed him. Ian wanted to be with her and you lost your family on Christmas because of it," he says and leans forward in his chair. "This isn't going to stop, he isn't going to stop unless we stop him."

She sniffs back her tears.

I.A.'s phone vibrates, he looks down at it and sees a message from Braden, his right-hand man. "Well, it looks like your problems are about to come to an end."

"What do you mean?"

"Ian just arrived at the hospital, Anthony is in place, and the girl is leaving. This might be all over sooner than you think."

Brigitte sniffs. "So, Flynn did as you asked?"

"Yes, did you doubt he would?" he asks sounding offended. "Listen, Brigitte, Anthony will move fast. You ordered this hit now you have to find a way to live with it...I need to go; I have my own problems to deal with."

"What do you mean I ordered this hit? I simply asked that you get Ellie out of Ian's life, I never asked you to kill her."

"Brigitte, how else do you expect me to get Ellie out of Ian's life?"

"Dad," Brigitte whispers.

I.A. release a loud sigh and his phone starts buzzing again. "I don't have time for this. Damian's men are on their way to Daniel and with any luck we will both be getting what we want."

"What do you mean?"

"I'm getting that ledger tonight, I'm ending this once and for all even if they have to torture Daniel's mother and father to get him to hand it over."

"I can't hear this."

"Oh, sweetheart, you already know too much. You'd better get used to the heat, you won't be going to heaven."

Brigitte swallows. "Are they going to kill them?"

I.A. shrugs with a devious smile. "If they have to. Daniel infiltrated Damian Santos Delabro's organization, learned the inner workings of his network, no one has ever done that before. No one has ever gotten that close before. Damian has no choice; besides, Daniel stole a large shipment of drugs and Damian can't let that go unpunished."

"Dad, I don't think you should get involved with this?"

"I'm already involved! Your brother, Angus, saw to that."

"But won't this trigger the release of evidence?"

"Yes, and if I have to kill Paul Logan I will."

Brigitte swallows hard, she's never heard him talk like this, never heard him talk about things like this. He has hinted to it, but he has never come right out to say it.

I.A. pours himself a scotch and exhales. "We need Ian, we need him focused and ready to take over in the event this all goes to bad. We need to get him under our control and with this girl out of the way we will."

She sighs and wonders if she shouldn't call her mother.

"Daniel has been blackmailing me for eighteen years, me and four others, that bastard has more than $2.5 million dollars of my money and I want it to stop."

"Dad, maybe we should take a step back and think about this."

"No," I.A. says shaking his head. "Listen, Brigitte, you wanted this, this is all on you, and you'd better keep your mouth shut. I won't tolerate another child of mine going against me."

Brigitte swallows and hangs up the phone. "Oh god," she cries and rests her head down on the counter as her daughter, Caroline walks in. "What have I done?"

Caroline looks at her mother, signs to her asking her what is wrong and when Brigitte looks up she simply shakes her head and signs back 'God help her'.

May 16 2008, 8PM

Standing in front of the large picture window behind his desk, overlooking the Capitol, Senator Hall sips his scotch and wonders what is going on when his cell phone vibrates.

"Hall..."

"I.A., Daniel got away."

"What?!"

Lara Stuart sighs. "Delabro's men had him and then, without warning, someone came to Daniel's rescue, attacked Delabro's men and two of them have been taken into custody."

"Oh god."

"I.A., Daniel knows you and Damian were behind this."

"That's ridiculous! How could he know I had anything to do with it?"

"Anthony was there."

I.A.'s face falls. "What?"

"We don't know why, but Daniel got away and he knows Anthony was there."

I.A.'s jaw clenches tight. "What about the girl?"

"I don't know. Anthony hasn't responded to my calls."

"Son of a bitch!" he shouts and throws his across the room and watches it hit the wall.

May 16 2008, 9:30PM

I.A.'s evening meeting ends just as his private cell phone begins to vibrate and when he sees who is calling, he gets up and leaves abruptly.

"Anthony! Where in the hell are you? What's happened?"

"It's done," Anthony mumbles. "The girl has been seriously injured, she's in the hospital. It doesn't look good."

"Where are you?"

"That doesn't matter. I'm going underground until this all dies down."

"Until what dies down? What is going on?"

"I'll be in touch," Anthony says and ends the call.

I.A. looks down at his phone and makes another call. "Braden! Anthony called, he says the girl is in the hospital. Did you block Ian's cell phone?"

"Yes, I blocked and hacked into both Ian's phone as well as the girl's. We can see everything they do and block whatever needs to be blocked."

"Good."

May 16 2008, 11:48 PM

Weary and unsure about what has happened, I.A. steps out of his garage and into his garden terrace behind his four-story row house in Georgetown when he sees a man sitting on a chair in the dark.

Stopping dead in his tracks, wishing Braden was there, he swallows. "May I help you?"

The man looks up, slowly withdraws the cigar from his mouth and looks at I.A.

"Damian," I.A. says sounding shocked. "What are you doing here?"

Damian sighs, leans forward to tap his cigar into a dish on the outdoor coffee table in front of him and six men step out from the shadows to surround him. "Have a seat," he says in a thick Spanish accent.

I.A. hesitates and suddenly there is a large hand on his shoulder forcing him to sit down and then the man moves to stand directly behind him making sure I.A. sees the gun in his holster.

Damian leans back and takes a drag off his cigar. "Two of my men were taken into custody tonight, one is on the run, but it will only be a matter of time before he is caught."

"What happened?" I.A. asks sounding genuinely concerned.

Damian looks at him. "You don't know? How could you not know?" he asks glaring at I.A. with a dangerous look on his face.

I.A. swallows.

Damian stands. "My men had Daniel, they were interrogating him, they were on the verge of finding out where my drugs are and where your ledger is, when a car drove into them, pinned them up against a wall and held them there until Daniel could crawl into the backseat!" he shouts and slams his hand down on the outdoor dining table.

I.A. swallows. "Who was it?"

Damian stands. "You have twenty-four hours to find out."

I.A. shakes his head. "What do you expect me to do? I have no idea who it was."

Damian stands and walks over to I.A. with his cigar in his hand and looks at it. "My men are now in your American jail. They understood the dangers of working for me, but they were not prepared for this."

I.A. looks up at him and then he looks back at the burning end of that cigar. "I don't know what happened, I swear."

Damian looks at him. "You need to find out."

I.A. shakes his head.

Damian squats down in front of I.A., nods toward two of his men who immediately lunge forward and grab I.A.'s left hand, turn it palm up, and wait. "I think you need a little reminder of who you are dealing with," he says and puts out the cigar in the palm of I.A.'s hand, holds it there and watches I.A. squirm. "Find out who did this and make sure they never see the light of day again...or I'll be back," Damian finishes putting out the cigar on I.A.'s hand and stands to leave. "Handle it."

I.A. watches them leave and so does his housekeeper. The moment she sees they are gone she runs out to help him, brings him inside and tends to his hand.

"I need to get to Lake Forest."

May 17 2008, 8:30AM

Brigitte pulls up to the pick-up area outside the main terminal and helps I.A. put his bags in the trunk when she notices his hand.

"What happened?"

He looks at her. "A warning from Damian Santos Delabro."

Brigitte's eyes widen. "A warning about what?"

I.A. ushers her into the car. "Daniel is missing."

Brigitte signals to pull away from the curb and shakes her head. "I knew this was going to blow up in our faces, I just knew."

I.A. shakes his head. "Shut up, Brigitte. I don't want to hear it. We need to find out what happened to Daniel, I need to find out where Anthony is and I need to know about this girl."

Brigitte shrugs. "Ian hasn't said a word."

I.A. sighs. "Delabro's men were dealing with Daniel when a car drove into them and pinned Delabro's men up against a brick wall. We have no idea who it was, but Daniel escaped in the car."

"Oh god."

"Delabro's men opened fire, struck the driver at least once."

"Oh god, do you have any idea who it is?"

I.A. shakes his head. "Two of Delabro's men are in custody, one is on the run. I need to find out what happened, I need to find Anthony, and I need to get out of town."

"What about me?"

"You are on your own."

"What about Ian?"

"I'm taking him with me."

Brigitte pauses. "He won't go."

I.A. looks at his daughter. "He has no choice."

"But Dad, I don't think Ian can. What about his residency?"

He looks at her. "You let me worry about that. If Damian gets hold of Ian he will use him to get to me. I keep Ian with me and he won't win," he says.

An ice-cold shiver runs down Brigitte's spine. "What about the rest of the kids? What about Andrew?"

"You need to figure it out. The only one I'm worried about is Ian."

"Dad!"

I.A. turns to look at her. "Do whatever you have to do, but make sure Ian leaves with me. Let's go!"

www.ingramcontent.com/pod-product-compliance
Lightning Source LLC
Chambersburg PA
CBHW060424130626

46555CB00005B/2210